Albert Dresden Vandam

Masterpieces of Crime

Albert Dresden Vandam

Masterpieces of Crime

ISBN/EAN: 9783743435537

Printed in Europe, USA, Canada, Australia, Japan

Cover: Foto ©Andreas Hilbeck / pixelio.de

Manufactured and distributed by brebook publishing software (www.brebook.com)

Albert Dresden Vandam

Masterpieces of Crime

MASTERPIECES OF CRIME

TOLD BY

ALBERT D. VANDAM

Author of 'The Curse of Desdemona,' 'A Coroner's Story,
'We Two at Monte Carlo,' etc.

EDEN, REMINGTON & CO., PUBLISHERS

LONDON AND SYDNEY

1892

CONTENTS

	PAGE
A French 'Jack the Ripper'	1
A Case of Forged Bank-Notes	30
A Past-Master in Crime	67
The Secret of the Guillotine	99
In Love's Disguise	127
Predecessors of Wainwright	157
An Anonymous Masterpiece	209
A Masterly Début	236
A Joint-Masterpiece	277

MASTERPIECES OF CRIME

A FRENCH 'JACK THE RIPPER'

In the morning of October 12, 1861, a girl, inscribed on the registers of the Paris Prefecture of Police as *une fille soumise*—which designation we leave the readers to translate for themselves—was found murdered in her room. The throat was cut from ear to ear, but one of the medical experts attached to the Criminal Investigation Department stated that death had ensued from strangulation, consequently the wounds inflicted on Jeanne Héris might be considered as a work of pure supererogation if the motive of the crime was merely robbery. When, four years ago, London was stirred to its depths by the exploits of the fiend in human shape whose name we shall probably never know, the theory of robbery had to be discarded at once. His victims belonged to the lowest class of 'unfortunates,' whose penury in England is proverbial. But in France even that lowest class, and to it Jeanne Héris undoubtedly belonged, gathers store, as will be seen by-and-by. It was, however, never ascertained whether she had been robbed; but this much was certain, that the murderer might have robbed her without the fear of being disturbed by her. Hence the mutilation of the body was gratuitous, the crime assumed a novel aspect, and the police were correspondingly puzzled. Neverthe-less, it would be an exaggeration to say that Paris was violently excited; nor did a similar murder, occurring eleven months later, produce any very great consterna-tion. Marguérite Lavie belonged to the same category of outcasts, and met with her death in the same manner as Jeanne

Héris. The police were as completely baffled in the one instance as in the other; but, wiser in their generation than our London detectives, they frankly acknowledged that they had no clue, and did not keep the public on the tenterhooks of expectation.

Nearly eighteen months elapsed. Jeanne Héris and Marguérite Lavie had been completely forgotten by the public, and were but faintly remembered by the detectives, when, on the 4th of February, 1864, another outcast named Lenoël was found frightfully mutilated in the room she occupied in one of the rookeries which have been demolished since to make way for the splendid thoroughfare, beloved by English and American tourists, the Avenue de l'Opéra. This time the capital was thoroughly aroused, and when, as in the two previous cases, the police had to confess their inability to trace the murderer, it clamoured for their dismissal *en masse*. As a matter of course, they might just as well have clamoured for the dismissal of Napoleon III himself, and perhaps with more success, had they been able to take things in their own hands; but, to do the late Emperor justice, he virtually joined in the outcry. Monsieur Claude, the head of the detective force, was sent for to the Tuileries, but, notwithstanding his tried ability, he confessed himself unable to cope with the matter. All he could allege with any degree of certainty was that the three crimes had been committed by the same hand, with the same daring, and accompanied by the same precautions not to leave behind the instrument with which the murders had been perpetrated. 'If,' he said, ' we had the most minute description of the murderer, and if that description pointed to the most phenomenal cast of countenance and the most misshapen body, we should not be able to pick him out from among a million and a half of people unless he belonged to the habitual criminal classes; and I am personally convinced that he does not belong to these. He is a monomaniac, but at ordinary times as sane as other people. Accident, and accident alone, will bring him into our hands.' Subsequent events proved that Monsieur Claude had taken the exact measure of the situation. Accident, and accident alone, brought Joseph Philippe to his doom, and that in spite of the fact of at least three women being in a position to give a description of him three or four weeks later on. They did not do so from fear of his vengeance, and only came forward when they knew he was powerless to harm them. We fancy this would not have been the case in England. As we proceed we shall have occasion to remark upon the general reluctance of the French to assist the police, and will explain the reason.

Still, there is little doubt, and notwithstanding M. Claude's pessimism, that, had timely warning been given by one, if not by both of the women who suspected Philippe's diabolical craving for human blood about a month later on, a few human lives might have been saved. On the 1st of March of the same year he accosted Hélène Meurand, who consented to let him accompany her home. She repented, however, almost immediately afterwards, and, leaving the stranger in her room, went downstairs and handed an inmate of the house her savings, amounting to thirty francs, alleging that she did not like the look of her visitor. She was not mistaken in her forebodings, for the latter tried to strangle her, and she only escaped the fate of the others by her stout resistance. She had been on her guard all the while, and at the first sign of Philippe's real intentions cried out lustily. He calmly took his leave. But instead of informing the authorities she kept silent, merely warning another girl of the same class. In fact, strange as it may seem when read by the light of subsequent revelations, the majority of these unfortunates round about that particular quarter, the Rues du Mail and St Joseph, appear to have had an inkling that the man 'wanted by the police' for the murders of Héris, Lavie, and Lenoël, and the night prowler of whom they stood in sufficient dread to refuse his advances, even when backed by comparatively liberal offers of money, were one and the same person; yet not one of them took the trouble to inform the police. Nay, when on April 15, a fourth victim is found to have been added to the list, a girl named Morgand carefully refrains from telling anyone that two days before the murder (April 10) she had met with Philippe, who began to be well known about the neighbourhood, and that she refused to have anything to say to him.

Julie Robert, the fourth victim, though in no way superior to the class from which the other three had been selected, appears to have been somewhat better off. She had a home of her own, a well-stocked linen press, which, moreover, contained over £50 in bank notes. This confirms my previous remark about the providence of even that class in France. The wardrobe was partly overhauled, but the money escaped detection, owing probably to its having been shifted from one shelf to another, and to the reluctance of the murderer to stay any longer. He might have done so with impunity, for the body was only discovered full sixty hours afterwards, and then only through a mere fortuitous circumstance. Julie Robert had arranged to move on that day, and the carman who called for that purpose gave the first alarm. But for this, a week or a month might have elapsed without anyone being the wiser. And yet Frenchmen will tell the foreigner who objects to the institution of the *concierge* that he is the guardian angel of one's life and property. A friend of mine, who is fond of paradox, and who has lived for many years in Paris, maintains that the best way of enlisting your *concierge's* vigilance with regard to your life and property is to owe always a quarter's rent to your landlord.

But Julie Robert was a girl who paid her way, consequently the *concierge* 'had seen nothing, heard nothing, knew nothing'; and the police were baffled as usual. It should be remembered that, unlike the London murders, these were perpetrated indoors; the chances of accidentally coming upon the miscreant, of catching him in the act, were considerably decreased; the more that there was evidence throughout of his having carefully washed the blood off his hands and clothes.

All kinds of measures were proposed, but Monsieur Claude shook his head dolefully. 'A hundred patrols of either amateur or professional detectives will not catch him,' he said, in answer to a suggestion to that effect. 'I will tell you what will happen. He will tire you out, and when next he appears it will be in quite a different quarter, and this will not be for many months. I have nothing to go upon, not even the knife or a handkerchief or a hat. The case is hopeless. He has not even an accomplice who might betray him.'

Monsieur Claude was right. Four months did elapse, and then the murderer had shifted the scene of operations from the centre of Paris to the north-eastern limits. Marie Helié was found on August 11 under circumstances similar to those of the other victims. There were the same marks on the throat, there was the same horrible gash from ear to ear, etc., etc. ; in short, it seemed as if the murderer was bent upon boldly throwing down the gauntlet to the police.

A veritable panic spread through the city ; and, as in London, the lowest class of outcasts plied their pitiful trade in fear and trembling. To this panic was due a description of the murderer, the first gleam of light vouchsafed to the detective force. Not that it proved of any avail; Monsieur Claude had an accurate perception of its value when he qualified it as 'a farthing rushlight in a cathedral.'

Between six and seven on Sunday morning, November 6, of the same year, the inmates of one of the tenements in the Rue Ste. Marguérite, in the Faubourg St Antoine, heard terrible cries issue from one of the rooms on the second floor. The Rue Ste. Marguérite and its vicinity was then and is still one of the two intra-mural headquarters of the rag-picking fraternity, the members of which are not addicted to settling their matrimonial and other differences *pianissimo*; consequently shrieks in one or more trebles, accompanied by the crash of broken crockery, excite little or no surprise, and provoke no active interference from the willing or unwilling listeners. Nor did they depart from their usual attitude this time, although the heart-rending appeals of a child rang above the shrieks of a woman. Ten minutes later a party of workmen passing below notice at an open window a female figure frantically holding on to the sill and uttering terrific yells. As they look up, something moist drips on their faces, and on their wiping it off they perceive it to be red. 'She began drinking early,' they say, taking it to be wine, and proceed on their way. A little while afterwards the *concierge*, sweeping the passage, finds a key in a heap of rubbish at the foot of the stairs, and hands it to Madame Mage's 'lover in ordinary,' who happens to come in at the same moment. 'That's how keys get lost,' she says, but without any further reference to the shrieks she, like everyone else in the house, must have heard, and to which she has remained just as indifferent.

I forbear describing the scene that met

the man's eyes, and which was given in full in the Paris newspapers next day. The struggle between the woman and her murderer must have been terrific, for a cat which happened to be in the bed was crushed to death against the wall. The mother and the child were literally hacked to pieces ; 'the blood,' says an eye-witness, ' lay in positive pools.' As usual, the murderer had rifled the woman's linen-press, carried off her small valuables and money, but had been careful not to leave anything behind that might afford a clue to the police. Still, within forty-eight hours of the last crime the latter were in possession of a detailed description of the man supplied by Josephine Fouché, who was within an ace of becoming a victim of Philippe on that Saturday night. There is no doubt that, like his successor in England, Philippe's thirst for blood increased as he went on, and that he intended to quench it if possible at two or three different sources at the same time. I give the girl's written statement almost in her own words; and supplement it by her evidence at the trial later on.

'Last Saturday,' she writes to the police on November 8, 'at about eleven, a man dressed in a blouse accosted me in the Rue Ste. Marguérite, close to where I live, and asked me to take him home with me. The moment we got into my room he wanted to give me his silver watch and chain and a 20 fr. piece. As he had no other money except a 2 fr. piece, he asked me to get change. I did not want to go down by myself, and did not want to put the key inside the door, seeing that he had already got into bed. I made him get up, saying that I did not feel well, and was thirsty. I was really shaking all over, but it was with fear. My individual trembled almost as much as I did. He seemed to be uncomfortable; he had something on his mind. I was the more afraid of him, seeing that I am not in good health and by no means strong. That is what pro-

bably attracted him after having talked to
Madame Mage. But I had my suspicions,
for when he spoke to me I noticed that he
seemed to hide something by the side of his
pocket, something hard and long. When I
went down to the wine-shop with him, the
proprietress of which is my landlady, I took
the opportunity of slipping away while he
ordered something to drink. I beckoned to
my landlady, who understood that I was
afraid. She gave me a candle, and made me
go through the private passage, saying,
" Get you to bed." She made him believe
that I lived with her. I was afraid; his
scowling looks, his dark complexion, slightly
pockmarked, the scar across his face, his
frizzy hair, and moustache chilled me to the
bone. But what frightened me most was
the tattoo-mark on his left arm—a flower,
with the words, " Born under an unlucky ' —
and then a star to finish the sentence.'

So far her first statement. When Philippe
was arrested, she was lying in the hospital

with some terrible disease of the eyes, and
when confronted with him recognised him
immediately. She virtually added little to
the letter, except when asked by the magistrate who was charged with taking her
evidence why she was frightened. She said
that she could not exactly account for her
fear, except that at the moment when he
got into bed his face assumed a diabolical
expression, and that at the same time she
caught sight of the mark on his arm. She
was under the impression that he was a
liberated convict, and she naturally 'shrank
from contact with such a man.' 'That's
why I avoided the brute who was so
fatal to my pal and her kid' (*ma farudole
avec son gosse*), she wound up. 'I have
shed many a bitter tear over this, and I
shall be very happy when I see his nut drop
into the sawdust' (*quand je verrai son
mufle moujioner, dans le son*). The sawdust
means the basket placed by the guillotine.
Josephine Fouché imagined that if she had

not rejected Philippe's overtures her companion Mage would have escaped her doom. She had seen him speak to the latter first and then turn to her. After the scene in the wine-shop she went upstairs and looked out of the window watching Philippe, who returned to Florence Mage. To us who have the exploits of 'Jack the Ripper' to go by, the conclusion of Fouché is by no means proven, and we are the more confirmed in our opinion that Philippe meant to kill two women that night by the evidence of the specialists previous to the trial, who maintained that these fits of erotic, homicidal mania gradually grow in length, and that one victim no longer suffices to assuage them.

Many months were to elapse before Philippe's head dropped into the sawdust. 'A farthing rushlight in a cathedral,' Monsieur Claude said when Fouché's letter was given to him. His opinion was shared by one of the cleverest examining magistrates the French Criminal Bench has known, Monsieur du Gonet, with whom we shall probably meet again in these papers. For the public, getting wind of Fouché's revelations, insisted through its organs that now the police's task was comparatively easy. Messieurs Claude, and Du Gonet's answer had better be pondered by the self-appointed critics of the police in all countries. 'The task is easy, you say,' they retorted. 'So it will be if you promise us not to raise an outcry at our apprehending every dark-complexioned, sinister-looking individual who is slightly pockmarked, who happens to have a scar across his face, who has frizzy dark hair, a thick, dark moustache and goatee. Of course we shall be permitted to go to the balls and receptions at the Tuileries, and wherever we like; for though the robbery that invariably accompanied these murders appears to be *primâ facie* evidence of their perpetrator being a poor man, this evidence the medical experts will tell you, is by no means conclusive. He may suffer from threefold complicated mania —erotic homicidal mania is already complex —in other words, depredatory mania may crown all his other enviable qualities. There is another way of facilitating the task of the police. Let the Legislature pass a sumptuary law, compelling every male adult to wear sleeves not reaching more than two or three inches below the shoulder, so that we may be able to ascertain at a glance whether the man is tattooed. We must have power at the same time to enter every house, for it is on the cards that the individual so distinguished will keep out of the streets.'

The retort was not only clever, but also logical. Unfortunately, the great publicity given to it must, to a certain extent, have neutralised the effects of the information acquired by the police. I consider M. Macé the cleverest detective chief the French have had for years. I knew him very well during his tenure of office, and am still on very friendly terms with him when I go to Paris; I also knew his predecessors, M. Jacob and M. Claude. With the latter I had several interviews twenty-two years ago. Well, they all three agreed that the Press can do a great deal of good if it consents to be guided in its accounts. Unlike their English colleagues, they never placed any difficulty in the way of the intelligent journalist; nay, they often invited his co-operation. Canler, Claude's predecessor, owed one of his cleverest strokes to the aid of the Press. They all maintained that there is no more assiduous reader of the accounts of his crime than the criminal himself, and that, therefore, the greatest discrimination should be exercised. The editor should take their hints. In the case of Philippe the editor did not; Philippe became aware of his description being published throughout the length and breadth of the land, and he held his murderous hand for more than fourteen months. When he

did operate again it was in an entirely
new quarter, and with a boldness that excited nearly as much admiration as horror.

The Faubourg St Honoré in the heyday
of the Second Empire was a much more
aristocratic neighbourhood than it is now,
and the Rue Ville l'Evêque was considered
one of its best streets. But the reader who
is even moderately acquainted with Paris
life from descriptions need not be told that
the juxtaposition of poverty and wealth,
of squalor and splendour, is nowhere so close
as in the ordinary Paris dwelling even in
the best parts of the town. No. 54 was,
however, by no means palatial; it was a
modest dwelling, inhabited by lower middle-
class folk, minor Government employés of
the Ministry of the Interior—the back entrance to which is in the thoroughfare
itself—'lean annuitants,' as Charles Lamb
said, etc. At the end of the courtyard was
the office of the Commissary of Police of
the district; a staircase under the gateway

led to the sets of apartments looking out upon the street. In a small set on the second floor lived Victoire Marie Bodeux, somewhat better off, perhaps, than the majority of her class, but in no way distinguished from them either in manners or appearance. On the third floor in a similar set of rooms lived a retired tradesman of more than seventy, named Maloiseau. His relations with Victoire Bodeux dated twenty years back. He appears to have been much attached to her, but nevertheless allowed her to pursue her shameful avocation. There are certain phases of life in all great capitals, but more especially in Paris, of which, unless one be writing a treatise on comparative morality, it behoves one to speak with bated breath.

On the evening of January 8, about eleven, Victoire Bodeux appears to have met with her murderer in the Rue Ville l'Evêque itself. A sentry on duty at the back entrance of the Ministry of the Interior subsequently spoke

to having seen them enter the house together, 'and,' added the soldier, 'it looked
as if the man was familiar with the place, for
he went first!' About an hour and a half
afterwards Maloiseau knocked at the office
of the Commissary of Police—which is not
a police-station in our sense of the word—
and informed the official that Victoire
Bodeux had been murdered in her apartments. The sight as they entered the room
was a ghastly one. The body still warm,
was lying on the floor of the second room ;
Victoire Bodeux had evidently been strangled
first, for her face had turned black, then her
throat had been cut from ear to ear. The
rugs were soaked in blood, the blood-stained
sheets and pillow-cases had been dragged
from the bed, the wardrobe and chest of
drawers forced. In short, everything attested a violent struggle between the victim
and her murderer. Before rifling the place
the latter had carefully washed his hands,
because there was not a single mark of

bloody fingers on any of the furniture, while on the washhand-stand stood a basinful of pinkish water. Still, the murderer had not been as careful as usual, for he had left behind the razor with which the wounds had been inflicted.

Suspicion fell at first on Maloiseau, but apart from the fact of Victoire Bodeux being an exceedingly robust woman—she was only thirty-eight—and her old admirer being the reverse, Maloiseau at once offered to take the police to his own apartment, and to prove an alibi if necessary. The authorities did not think it necessary, and accepted the statement he volunteered in good faith. He had spent the evening with some friends, and got home a few minutes after twelve, when he had knocked at Victoire Bodeux's door. Receiving no answer, he had instinctively turned the handle of the door which led immediately to the sitting-room preceding the bed-room. The door was not locked, and, on its yielding, he saw a stranger arranging

his necktie before the looking-glass. Thereupon Maloiseau had discreetly retired, in-
tending to return in a little while. When
he did return he was confronted by the
spectacle above described.

There was no need on the part of the
police to indulge in suppositions as to the
identity of the murderer. Every fact
pointed to its having been perpetrated by
the hand that had slain all the other outcasts. The razor afforded no clue ; it bore
a merely stereotyped trade-mark ; thousands
of a similar shape and make were no doubt
in existence. Nor was the fact of Victoire
Bodeux having been robbed, among other
things, of a purse containing 100 fr. in
gold of any avail. The purse was a present
from Maloiseau. The purse would be a clue
when found, but it had to be found first.

The police confessed themselves as powerless as ever, when on January 11, in broad
daylight, a man was arrested in the Faubourg St Germain. He was apparently

running away from his pursuers when a policeman on duty at the corner of the Rue Jacob tripped him up. Taken to the police-station and searched, there was found upon him a long, sharp table-knife and a small bolster-case, made of grey ticking. He had a very soldierly bearing, and was not above thirty-five. He was charged with an attempt to murder and rob Madame Midy, an artist, living in the Rue d'Erfurt. Madame Midy was a customer of his former employer, a framemaker and gilder named Dangleterre, in the Rue de Seine. Having rung at Madame Midy's studio, and the door having been opened by the lady herself, he pretended that on a former occasion he had lost a tool, and had come to look for it. Having got inside the place, he pulled the bolster-case from his pocket, and asked Madame Midy whether she could identify the article as her own. The lady, annoyed at his intrusion on so shallow a pretext had turned to her easel. Thereupon

the man had flung the case over her head,
and, holding one hand over her mouth, had
tried to strangle her with the other.
Madame Midy dropped to the ground, and
in her desperate efforts to free herself from
her assailant bit one of his fingers through
and through.

A fellow-artist, whose studio was divided
from hers by a thin partition heard her cries
of distress, and tried to come to the rescue,
but the door was locked. His ring at the
bell remaining unanswered, he ran to the
window on the landing and shouted for the
concierge, and knocked at the door again.
This time it was opened by an individual
who quietly walked past him, saying, 'Do
not trouble yourself; she is ill. I am going
for the doctor.' Wherewith he as quietly
walked down stairs. But Madame Midy,
who had slightly recovered, shouted, 'Stop
him, stop him!' Some inmates of the house
gave chase, and Joseph Philippe was pulled
up at the corner of the Rue Jacob.

For some hours after his arrest there was not the slightest suspicion that the man who had terrorised Paris for four years or more had been caged at last. It was only when his room was searched that the suspicion dawned upon Monsieur Claude. 'From that moment, and from that moment only,' he said afterwards, 'our task became easy.' And though the case took nearly five months in 'getting up' (the French verb is *instruire*, and means the examination of the prisoner and witnesses by the *juge d'instruction*, which functionary has not his counterpart in England) there was not the slightest doubt as to the guilt of Joseph Philippe.

The most damning proofs against him with regard to crimes prior to the murder of Victoire Bodeux were the statement of the girl Fouché, and the evidence of a laundress and of a needlewoman. The one deposed to having washed his blood-stained clothes, the second to having hemmed a towel found in his room for Julie Robert. Philippe opposed a denial to most things, still his demeanour was not undignified. Several of his former employers testified to his being a good servant when sober It was drink that began his ruin and developed the erotic, homicidal mania until it became irresistible. His appearance when in the dock tallied exactly with Josephine Fouché's description. He was sentenced to death on June 28, 1866, and executed in the middle of July. He met his fate like a man; in fact, Monsieur Claude and several eminent specialists who had carefully studied him during his incarceration gave it as their opinion that under the circumstances, 'he was glad to die,'—that life, shorn of its usual debauches, would be irksome to him.

A CASE OF
FORGED BANK-NOTES

DETECTIVE SUPERINTENDENT, or, to give him
his German title, Criminal Commissary,
Carl Weien sat wrapt in a brown study.   He
felt 'small' as our American cousins have it.
Having made murder and burglary, etc., his
special business, he had in an evil hour
engaged in a trial of skill with a gang of
forgers and utterers of false bank-notes, and
up to the present had been signally worsted.
For nine months they had kept him at bay,
baffled all his researches, while continuing to
inundate Berlin and the neighbourhood with
their spurious 'five-mark' notes.   During
the first seven months of the year 1879 not

a day elapsed without three or four complaints reaching the central office in the
Molkenmarkt. True, for the last two
months these complaints had almost entirely
ceased, but Superintendent Weien did not
deceive himself as to the causes of this cessa-
tion. He did not for a single moment
imagine that the gang had abandoned their
game either from fear or because they had
amassed a competency; they had simply
suspended operations in order to fortify their
position—in other words, to rectify the few
flaws that marred their production. The
first and foremost of these was, the shade of
blue employed in the hatching, which was a
trifle too deep, though sufficiently near the
mark to deceive any but the most careful
examiner, especially at first sight and in a
doubtful light. The latter advantage, from
their point of view, had been almost invariably secured by the utterers of these forged
notes. They generally selected their victims
from among the small tradesmen, whose

establishments at the best of times were in semi - darkness. Their favourite time of operation was, moreover, at dusk; but, as I have already said, it wanted a very practised eye to detect their forgeries even on the brightest day, because the forger's constant use of the same figures and letters would fail to strike those not in the habit of handling a great many notes. And comparatively small as was the supposed value of the shams—a mark represents exactly a shilling of our coin—the recipients did not turn over sufficiently many genuine ones to distinguish at a glance between the two.

Though the authorities had not succeeded in catching a single one of the gang in the act, Superintendent Weien was not without his suspicions as to the identity of the principal offender — namely, the actual forger. Truly, Weien's suspicion was mainly an instinctive one. There was not the slightest material proof against the man;

but there were several convictions recorded
against him for similar crimes. In this
respect he was one of many, but apart
from the fact of his standing as a copper-
plate engraver a head and shoulders taller
than the most skilful of his craft, his deft-
ness with the needle almost amounting to
genius, he of all those suspected and watched
at first had given his watchers the slip.
Lomnitz—that was the man's name—was
sixty : five-and-twenty years of which had
been spent in different prisons for forging
bank-notes. During one of those terms of
imprisonment at Spandau he had engraved
some marvellous military maps for the
Grand-General Staff; he had, moreover,
constructed a sliding-gauge for the artillery,
which had proved so useful that the War
Office sent him a gratuity of 60 thalers
(£9). In short, Lomnitz was one of those
criminals whom the novelist is often taxed
with inventing, while in reality the novelist
tones down the authenticated facts, lest he

should not be believed by the most credu-
lous of readers.

Lomnitz had been watched for six months
by the myrmidons of Superintendent Weien,
who, though morally certain of his complicity in the recent forgeries was, for
various reasons, reluctant to apprehend him.
First of all, Weien was not only anxious to
arrest the maker of the notes, but to get
possession also of the whole of the apparatus
and material, and it was very evident that
the latter would not be found in either of
the two domiciles Lomnitz had successively
occupied from January till June—the period
when he had disappeared.   Secondly, the
gang was apparently a numerous one, and
the organisation well planned and equally
well carried out; and yet during the six
months of Lomnitz's surveillance he had
scarcely held communication inside or outside his dwelling with anyone, and least
of all with anyone at whom suspicion
pointed in the remotest way   Lomnitz

lived very quietly and retired, apparently provided for by his well-to-do and respectable children, established in one of the suburbs. Weien, being determined to make a clean sweep of the whole gang, bided his time and held his hand. While the detective was weighing pros and cons, Lomnitz disappeared.

Three months had elapsed since then, and not the faintest trace of Lomnitz had been discovered, though Weien's most trusty and clever agents had absolutely explored the capital and its outskirts in all directions. At the same time the operations seemed to have been suspended, but, as I have said, the energetic and able detective was not hoodwinked by this, nor induced to believe that the thing was at an end. The discovery of the plot had become a fixed idea with him, but, though fully bent upon carrying it out, he could not help being disheartened now and then when, after recapitulating all he had done, he had to come to the reluctant conclusion that, unless chance befriended him, it would be so much time wasted.

His surroundings on that particular October afternoon were scarcely calculated to improve his drooping spirits. The Scotland-yard of Berlin was, and may be still —for it is four years since I saw it—the most dismal building ever devised by any architect. Long passages leading to small rooms in which the gas is never extinguished from one year's end to another, walls that look as if they had been daubed with a pigment composed of snuff and soft soap, carpetless floors, and worm-eaten rickety furniture depress the visitor, however innocent, to a degree such as to make him wonder whether he will ever issue from there a free and, if a free, a sane man.

The part devoted to the transaction of criminal business is, if anything, worse, and it was in one of its rooms that Superintendent Weien sat brooding on his failure.

He was on duty, which meant that he had
come at two that afternoon, and would not
leave until twelve o'clock next day, during
which time he was absolutely in charge,
dealing, in a certain way, with all those
brought in, besides receiving and examining
the batches of offenders arriving at frequent
intervals from the various police by 'Black
Maria,' which conveyance in Berlin is
painted a rather vivid green.

Before proceeding with my story I must
ask the reader to dismiss from his mind all
his previously conceived notions based upon
English criminal procedure. The Berlin
detective superintendent is invested with
very extensive powers. He is a magistrate
in so much that he has the right to examine
prisoners; he discharges the functions of an
ordinary inspector at a police-station, etc.
And far from being compelled to warn
prisoners that everything they say will be
used as evidence against them, he enjoys
the liberty of coercing or cajoling them into

admitting their guilt by any and every means short of corporal punishment. There are thirty of these superintendents in Berlin, each of whom is on duty one day during the month, though a good many are in and out the Molkenmarkt at all times, getting familiar in that way with the criminal population of the capital and gathering knowledge denied to their London colleagues. As we go on we will see what they may and may not do, and the advantages derived from the system so far as the detection of crime goes. Superintendent Weien was disturbed in his meditations by the entrance of a sergeant with a bundle of reports referring to a batch of prisoners from the green police-van. He had gone mechanically through half of them when he positively jumped from his chair. The following document lay before him :—

'Julius Barth, twenty-two years of age, professing to be an artisan, arrested and brought to the Madgeburg police-station, charged with being concerned in passing the apparently forged five-mark note, herewith. The presumption that the prisoner was aware of the forgery is based upon the fact of his trying to take flight, leaving the note behind, when the apprentice Roach, to whom the note was tendered, began to examine it carefully. He was pursued, and brought before the undersigned,

'J. TIMMER,

'Police Lieutenant M Division.'

Appended was the detailed report of the charge, from which it appeared that Julius Barth, when questioned as to how he got possession of the note, alleged having received it from a waiter in the Zoological Gardens among the change for a twenty-mark gold piece, which he had tendered in payment for refreshment.

The reader will pardon another short digression. In London or in any of the large cities Barth would never have got to the central office. He would have been locked up until next morning at the police-station whither he was brought at first; next morning he would have been charged before a police magistrate, and remanded for further inquiries or committed for trial; a few hours later the report of the proceedings at the police-court would have been in the papers. The detective engaged upon the case would probably have been left in the dark until then. Meanwhile the principals in the affair would have got scent of the capture and also taken their precautions. At any rate, the magistrate would have had no power to act as Weien did, and the police would have been as wise as ever. I do not pretend to comment, I merely state a fact.

Superintendent Weien had Barth brought to him at once. I do not overlook the fact that, had another superintendent been on duty, things would not have gone so smoothly, especially if the latter had also got an interest in the affair, which might have been ; but certain is it that even then Weien, if he had kept his eyes open, could and would have become acquainted with the report before it was made public, and that he would have had an equal right with all the other superintendents to interrogate Barth. Something else. Though the law provides for the hearing of a prisoner before a magistrate as soon as possible after his apprehension, a certain latitude is allowed.

Weien perceived at a glance that he was dealing with a novice in crime. Barth was poorly but cleanly dressed, and looked very frightened. Weien knew how to deal with the tyro as well as with the hardened criminal, and in a comparatively short time got the truth out of Barth. Barth had been out of work a long while, and in his wanderings in search of it had become acquainted with a house-painter in a similar predicament. For weeks they had gone about penniless, until one day, to Barth's great astonishment, Möller seemed to be comparatively flush of money. Pressed by Barth to explain, Möller had prevaricated a good deal, and at last confessed to the traffic in false notes, on each of which he gained a mark and a half. He got the notes from a man, an utter stranger. Möller knew neither his name nor where he lived, but he knew the hour and spot at which to meet him on certain days. Still, according to Barth, Möller's father and later on his (Barth's) landlord, became engaged in the same traffic, 'but we have been obliged to cease passing them for months, because one of the colours was too dark. The stranger did not get the notes direct from the makers, but through a middleman,' concluded Barth.

The latter statement tallied so exactly with what Superintendent Weien knew already as to induce him to credit the rest —at any rate, for the time being. Furthermore, the pause in the circulation, the exact date of which was specified by Barth, coincided exactly with the period when Lomnitz had been under the strictest surveillance, and when the agents reported that he held communication with no one and lived in the strictest retirement. That was the time when he was devising improvements.

The affair seemed to assume such dimensions as to make it necessary for Weien to communicate more fully upon the subject with his chief. The latter approved of what he had done hitherto, and recommended the strictest secrecy. Meanwhile Barth was placed at the disposal of the 'investigating magistrate,' who is the German equivalent for the French *juge d'instruction*, with whose functions the reader is sufficiently familiar The two Möllers were apprehended, for Weien rightly considered that if he failed to take that step the investigating magistrate, entrusted with Barth's case, or the Procurator-General would order their arrest. He furthermore considered that the arrest of two such subordinate personages in the case would have no deterrent effect either on the principals or on the more important intermediate factors.

In this he was to a slight extent mistaken, as will be apparent directly. The two Möllers at first denied their guilt, and stigmatised Barth's story as a pure invention; but they confessed at last, and the son gave a description of the man who supplied him with the notes. The description was, upon the face of it, a true one; the next thing was to find the man—if not to arrest, at least to watch him carefully. According to young Möller, he was about forty, well built, with fair hair and moustache. He wore dark clothes, and was upon the whole dressed like a gentleman. But there might be a few thousand such in the capital, and beyond Möller's additional statement as to the particular street whence the stranger invariably came to keep his appointments there was nothing to guide Weien.

Still, the discovery of the man was so thoroughly necessary to Weien's scheme that as he himself admitted, he engaged upon the almost forlorn hope of having the street indicated by Möller searched from one end to another. The search was, contrary to his expectation, crowned with a certain measure of success. One of the gossips of the neighbourhood fancied that in one of the back premises in said street there lived a man tallying with the description of the agents. His name was Kaumann, and he had been engaged in business. She did not know what he was doing then. A reference to the criminal records soon convinced Weien that Kaumann was an old acquaintance who had undergone several sentences for fraud and fraudulent bankruptcy. Kaumann therefore was no novice, and he had to be watched with great circumspection. Weien himself accompanied by two of his most trusty agents, and disguised as the worst kind of vagrants, prowled for several days and nights in the neighbourhood, and in the suburban road itself, where Möller and Kaumann had held their appointments, seeing that Weien was firmly convinced that he had not got hold of the tenth part of the subordinates in the affair. They enacted their *rôles* so well as to deceive the very mounted police, from whom they had to fly several times. Weien had recourse to several other stratagems, but they were all in vain. Kaumann was either on his guard in consequence of the arrest of the two Möllers, of which he had been informed by public rumour, or else Weien had followed the wrong scent; at any rate, he came to the conclusion that he had made a mistake in arresting Barth's companions too quickly or too openly. Nevertheless, it was certain that Kaumann was not in business at that present moment, and that notwithstanding he was living on the fat of the land.

After a week of this fruitless manœuvring
Weien made up his mind to resort to more
energetic, not to say desperate, measures;
for the attempt of a detective, no
matter how clever at disguising himself, to
come into personal contact with a real or
suspected criminal who is on his guard is
considered a desperate measure in the profession. The inspector selected for the
task was, however, one of the ablest men
in the service, though comparatively young.
He had gained admission into the force by
two of the cleverest strokes on record when
a mere auxiliary. His name was Feldau.

*   *   *   *   *

Towards dusk on the third or fourth day
after the events described above, a tall,
stalwart young fellow, apparently a plumber
by trade, walked into one of the most
notorious thieves' haunts in the old König-
stadt quarter. The establishment consisted

of a large front room fitted up as a kind of
café, with a billiard table in the centre, a
counter near the door, an old piano against
one of the walls, and several wooden tables,
flanked by rush-bottomed chairs, the whole
smoke-begrimmed and dirty to a degree.
The smaller room at the back seemed altogether untenanted.   At the first sight of
the new comer the conversation of the eight
customers in the room ceased as if by magic.
The game of billiards, upon which four
young and showily-dressed individuals were
engaged, was continued in silence, while at
the table, occupied by an old hag, a young
girl, looking prematurely old, and two un-
kempt, untidy, middle-aged men, not so
much as a whisper was heard.

The plumber took not the slightest notice
of this ominous silence, but shaking the
rain from off his clothes, and putting his
bundle of tools on a table near the door,
he sat down and ordered a particular kind
of dram known as *Nordhäuser Schnapps*.

He, however, did not make the mistake of calling it by that name, but simply said 'a *Nordlicht*.' To have designated it by any other appellation would have been admitting at once that he did not belong to the Berlin populace. Still, notwithstanding this voucher on his part, the chill thrown by his advent on the company did not thaw. They kept signalling to, and looking at one another significantly. The result of this mute conference, accompanied by very searching glances at his overalls, and especially at his hands, seemed favourable to the stranger, for the conversation was resumed. They seemed to have concluded that he was a harmless working-man, driven into their lair by stress of weather.

This opinion was endorsed by one of their own chums, who made his appearance about ten minutes later, and who was welcomed with demonstrations of delight. Had the company been less engrossed with their new companion, or resumed their scrutiny just then, they might have become aware of the plumber's eye lighting up with satisfaction at the fresh arrival. The latter, whom the company addressed as 'Hussar William,' but who was none other than Kaumann, seemed to be a great favourite, and generous with his money. He treated them all round, and kept them roaring with his funny stories. Now and then he cast a look at the plumber, who was examining his tools, like a man who does not know what to do with his time while waiting to proceed on his way. It had been raining in torrents, but it was clearing up; the plumber, whose glass had been empty for a quarter of an hour or more, had probably not the money to have it refilled; at any rate, he stared repeatedly at the other table, where the feasting went on uninterruptedly. Seeing which, Hussar William stepped up to him. 'Well, old pal,' he exclaimed in a cheerful voice—'plenty of work?'

The plumber scratched his ear and told his interlocutor that work was very slack; that to-morrow there would be an end of it as far as he was concerned, and that if the weather did not mend there was little prospect of getting any for some time. 'It means taking in the belt a hole or two,' he concluded in a somewhat doleful tone. At the reply Kaumann stared fixedly at him for a few seconds, but the workman took no notice, paid for his dram, and rose to go. Thereupon, Kaumann offered to stand treat, and drank his new acquaintance's good health, wishing him lots of business. When the latter had his hand on the door, Kaumann shouted to him to come again soon, he might be able to put a few marks in his way. The workman thanked him, and left the place.

For full a fortnight after this the plumber took his seat every day at dusk at that table near the door, where Kaumann invariably joined him. He seemed to have

taken a great liking to the simple-minded
workman, who told him all his affairs, while
he, Kaumann, confined himself to mere
commonplace remarks, inwardly chuckling
at the man's simplicity, though ever scan-
ning him carefully, to make thoroughly
sure that he was dealing with a fool, and
not with a knave. The plumber, on the
other hand, looked more woebegone each
day. Such household goods as he possessed
were fast disappearing, to feed his ailing
wife and four young children. Kaumann
seemed deeply affected by this tale of woe,
and quietly put a mark in his hand now
and then, telling him to 'keep his pecker
up.' One evening, as the plumber was
about to take his departure, Kaumann
offered to accompany him part of the way,
seeing that they were going in the same
direction. They had scarcely got in the
street when Kaumann opened his batteries.
He asked the plumber point blank whether
he had ever 'been in trouble.' The latter

merely hung his head, and muttered a few incoherent words in reply. Kaumann laughed, and told his companion there was no need to mince matters with him. That kind of thing might happen to anyone; he himself 'had done time' more than once. Encouraged by this open-heartedness, the plumber confessed to his own small sins. He had been in prison twice—a fortnight once, three months the second time. He had allowed his comrades to take away material from new buildings where he was working, and so forth. Kaumann laughed again, and inquired whether that was all. At any rate, he had something to propose which might bring his friend a couple of thalers a day. 'A couple of thalers a day!' gasped the poor wight, his eyes almost starting from their sockets. 'A couple of thalers a day!' he repeated; 'why, I would work my fingers to the bone.' Kaumann told him that there was no need to work his fingers to the bone, that, in fact, there was no need to work at all, and at last produced a five-mark note, ' with directions for use.'   In a short while he had prevailed upon the plumber, who seemed reluctant to engage upon the traffic, to have at any rate ' a try for the sake of his ailing wife and children.'   They parted, after having made an appointment at the tavern for the following evening.   Three hours later, Feldau, still in his workman's dress, gave Weien a full report of the affair at the latter's private dwelling.

It need scarcely be said that the next step on Weien's part was to watch Kaumann more strictly than ever, while Feldau continued to play his part as the plumber, pretending to get rid of the spurious notes and handing his ' benefactor ' the proceeds. Forty-eight hours after Feldau's supposed entry into Kaumann's plot he was able to report that the latter had appointed to meet the principal factor in the affair on the following evening.   Weien himself, aided by

Werner, another inspector, even more skilled than Feldau, took the field that night, with the result that at half-past nine on that same evening they had tracked the chief circulator of the notes to his lodgings, without, however, knowing his name. In a very short time, however, Weien found that he was dealing with an old and hardened offender, one Hubert Spangenberg.

*   *   *   *   *

Weien became at once aware that in Spangenberg he was confronted with a foeman well worthy of his steel. Spangenberg's latest offence dated from about nine years previously, before Weien's connection with the detective force. Seven of these had been spent in Spandau at the same time that Lomnitz was an inmate of that prison, though from the records it appeared that they were not implicated in the same offence. Though firmly convinced that Lomnitz, and Lomnitz only, was the perpetrator of the present forgeries, Weien was too experienced a criminal detective not to guard against being too sure, against refusing to follow another scent because it came second instead of first. Spangenberg's antecedents pointed to a connection with a firm of lithographers, the members of which also had been convicted. They were quietly arrested, but Spangenberg was left to pursue his course without being molested in the slightest. Of course he was watched day and night by Inspector Werner, whom I mentioned incidentally just now, and whose talent for disguising himself is still a topic of conversation in the Berlin detective force.

Spangenberg lived with his brother-in-law, a baker, who for the time had retired from business, and was keeping a kind of gambling hell exclusively for bakers, who are notorious gamblers. Some time ago the Berlin correspondent of a London contemporary drew attention to this fact. He was scarcely believed by his English readers. From personal observation I can testify that he understated rather than overstated the case.

Werner, after having watched for several weeks, and dogged Spangenberg's every footstep in various disguises, came to the conclusion that the supply of notes which he (Spangenberg) distributed among his emissaries was renewed inside and not outside the house, in which conclusion as we shall see directly, he was completely mistaken. He therefore tried to gain admission to the house, first by courting the servant maid in the guise of a tramway conductor; then in the guise of a waiter who was going to set up in business for himself. On this occasion he was introduced by an old schoolfellow who happened to be a baker, and whom he had seen coming out of the house. But he only succeeded in discovering one or two more utterers of the notes; of their maker there was not the slightest trace. It was very evident that there was no personal communication between him and Spangenberg. There was an intermediary, who might or might not be innocent of the part he was playing ; but who or what he was, how the transfer of the notes was effected, remained an enigma—an enigma apparently not nearer its solution in the beginning of December than it was in the beginning of November, when Weien tracked Spangenberg to his lodgings for the first time. All that Werner could with certainty affirm was that Spangenberg was a great admirer of 'the sex,' that he had frequent appointments with women who from their social position were not suspected of such escapades. The fair one to whom he seemed most attached, though, and to whom he paid frequent visits, was a young girl who lived with her mother, but who was known to be under the protection of a Berlin banker. For hours Werner watched the house while Spangenberg paid one of his periodical visits. Like most continental houses in large cities, it consisted of several flats, and was occupied by several families. Nevertheless, during that evening only one woman went in, and she left half-an-hour after. Nor did subsequent inquiries and even a personal visit from Werner, disguised as a messenger, reveal any facts connecting the mother and daughter with the emission of the forged notes. Spangenberg received many letters, but Werner had ascertained that they were mostly in female handwriting—love letters, as they afterwards turned out to be, for Spangenberg, though far from handsome, was what some women call 'interesting,' and, though he sprang from the humbler classes, had a distinguished appearance, which his manner did not belie.

*　　*　　*　　*　　*

The middle of December had come, and there was not the slightest trace of Lomnitz. His children had heard nothing of him. The earth seemed to have swallowed him up. And although Weien admitted to himself the possibility of having made a mistake in fastening the guilt upon Lomnitz, the very fact of the latter's unaccountable disappearance went far to strengthen the suspicion against him. And on the morning of December 20, Superintendent Weien sat once more in a brown study in one of the rooms in the Molkenmarkt. A few minutes afterwards he sent Werner for Lomnitz's 'criminal record.' Weien wanted to refresh his memory, with the hope perhaps of finding something new. Werner returned almost immediately with the astounding intelligence that Lomnitz's record had been inquired for half-an-hour previously by another superintendent, who had already consulted it more than once.

Weien sat like one thunderstruck. Others were engaged in the same affair, and too many cooks would infallibly spoil the broth. Apart from the fact that he (Weien) considered himself 'the man' to bring the affair to a conclusion in virtue of his having been so long engaged upon it, he feared that some ill-advised step on the part of the others might alarm Spangenberg, who would not fail to put the frontier between himself, Lomnitz, and the police. Such a contingency had to be prevented at all costs. Consequently he resolved upon the desperate measure of having Kaumann and Spangenberg arrested there and then. Werner was entrusted with the task of apprehending the first, Weien himself undertook to cage the other. A search at Spangenberg's house did not bring a single note to light; the only suspicious article found was a small bottle of blue fluid, apparently a kind of printing ink. As a matter of course, Spangenberg denied his guilt: he knew nothing of Lomnitz—had not seen him for years. Confronted with one of the lithographers, to whom we alluded before, nothing was elicited from either; but the latter averred that some days previous to his arrest he had met

Lomnitz in the neighbourhood of the Humboldshain. More than that he could not say. He was absolutely ignorant of the street in which Lomnitz lived. It was the faintest spark of light to Weien, but he resolved to act up to it there and then. It had been clear to him for some time that ' the workshop' was in the northern part of Berlin ; Kaumann and Spangenberg lived and met in that part, and nearly all those arrested up till now had their usual haunts there. One thing was certain ; that if he did not succeed in capturing Lomnitz that night, the bird would have flown in the morning, for though the police have some power with regard to the Press, they could not keep the report of so important an arrest as that of Spangenberg and Kaumann out of the papers.

❋   ❋   ❋   ❋   ❋

At seven o'clock that same evening Weien, accompanied by twenty detectives, started for ' the Pomeranian quarter,' which derives its title from the fact of each street being named after a town or village of that old province of Prussia. The score of detectives were divided into couples, and to each couple two streets were allotted in which to make inquiries from house to house. The description of Lomnitz was impressed upon every one ; they had further orders, in the event of their finding a trace, not to disturb him, but to send one man to a certain spot, agreed upon beforehand, to warn Weien himself, while the other kept watching the house. For three hours the search was attended with no result. It struck ten when Weien and his coadjutor left the last house in the Stettiner Strasse and turned into the Rügener Strasse. The front doors used not to be closed so punctually at ten as they are nowadays, and Weien, though utterly spent and disheartened, would leave no stone unturned. Towards half-past ten he entered one of the last houses still open and ascended to the first floor, where the Vizewirt (*concierge, housekeeper*) had his lodge. In answer to the inquiry, repeated perhaps for the thousandth time that night, the housekeeper shook his head in the negative; but his young daughter, after a moment's reflection, interrupted him. 'That must be Herr Wendt, right on the top, on the fourth floor. He does not rent his rooms directly from us; that's why father overlooked him. Besides, one scarcely sees him. He is a nice, kind old man, somewhat ailing, who would not hurt a cat.' 'A nice, kind old man, ailing and very weak, with white hair,' etc. The description tallied with that of Lomnitz. In another moment Weien, his heart jumping against his ribs, was at the top of the building, having left two of his companions posted on the first-floor landing.

Weien's first summons remained unanswered. At the second he heard a light step within, and in another moment a soft voice inquired, 'Who is there?' Without the least hesitation Weien whispered, 'Quick, for Heaven's sake, open the door!' And when the door was opened the fourth act of the drama was virtually at an end, the principal actor in it, nay, the author of it, had been run to earth. Nor for one moment did he attempt to deny his guilt. He behaved with the greatest dignity—a dignity that compelled admiration even from his captor. All his efforts were directed to exculpate those arrested with him—two Russians and his housekeeper, the woman to whom Werner had paid no attention on the night he had watched the house of Spangenberg's, chief *inamorata*. She had been the apparently innocent means of communication between Lomnitz and Spangenberg. She left a parcel every now and then at the house of the pretty Elise Merten, who was utterly ignorant of her lover's traffic, but who clung to him through thick

and thin, until, long before the expiration
of his sentence, the remainder of it was
commuted on the ground of insanity—
whether real or cleverly simulated it would
be difficult to determine.   At the time of
the Emperor Frederick's death (1888)
Spangenberg was living in poor circumstances in Berlin, supported by Elise Merten.
Lomnitz was still alive in Sonnenburg prison,
working out his sentence of ten years.   The
rest had already been discharged, and had
fallen into evil courses again.   Lomnitz's
housekeeper and the two Russians were
acquitted, mainly through Lomnitz's exer-
tions in their behalf.   He did not attempt
to defend himself.   Feldau and Werner
were awarded £15 each in recognition of
their services.   Weien received £40, and
rightly enjoys the utmost consideration at
the hands of his chief.

A PAST-MASTER IN CRIME

'EVERYTHING that happens has happened before,' said a mediæval rabbi of Toledo, 'and our astonishment at the actual event springs as a rule from our ignorance of similar ones that preceded it in the course of ages.'

The axiom was forcibly illustrated about three years ago, when two miscreants decoyed a postman into their rooms in Hatton Garden, for the purpose of getting hold of his 'first delivery,' which on that particular morning was likely to contain registered letters with very valuable contents. The attempt is too recent to need recapitulating at great length, and I only refer to it on account of the astonishment at 'the daring and bold originality of the scheme' expressed at the time by the glib descriptive reporter and the learned leader writer. Truly, their astonishment sprang from their ignorance of the name of Georges Lacenaire, who was to a certain extent the inventor of that kind of thing; to a certain extent, because 'the decoy lay' itself is as old as the hills. He only modified the conditions.

On December 29, 1834, an individual evidently on the point of taking a long journey called upon Messrs Maigre-Morstadt and Mallet, bankers in the Faubourg Poissonière, and entrusted them with the cashing of two bills of exchange, one of which was payable two days later at a Monsieur Mahossier's, 66, Rue Montorgueil. Towards half-past three in the afternoon of the 31st a bank porter named Genevey applied at the house indicated, and, after mounting four flights of stairs, found himself before the door of a back room, on which the name of 'Mahossier' was scribbled in chalk. He was exact to the minute, for the stranger who left the bills with the bankers had made it a point in his instructions that Monsieur Mahossier was only at home between a quarter-past three and a quarter to four. It was not difficult, by the light of subsequent events, to guess the drift of these instructions. At that late hour of the day Genevey would, in all probability, have upon him the whole of the sums collected during his round. In answer to his knock the door was opened immediately, and closed as quickly. Save for two trusses of straw and a large basket with a deal board atop of it, the room was absolutely bare of furniture. Two men were waiting for the bank porter; one of them struck him a severe blow with a sharp instrument between the shoulder blades, trying at the same time to get hold of his leather case containing 10,000 francs in notes, and his satchel containing 1100 francs in gold, while the other placed his hand on Genevey's mouth to prevent his shouting. The hosts this time had reckoned without their guest, who, though but eighteen years of age, and seriously wounded, offered a desperate resistance, and succeeded in shaking off both his assailants, shouting lustily for help all the while. Finding themselves baffled, the latter took flight, and succeeded in making their escape. These were the scanty particulars that reached the Prefecture of Police, nor did a careful examination of the room reveal any more than that; the instrument with which the wound had been inflicted—a long stiletto—bearing no maker's name, and the basket and the board failing to afford the least clue. For nine days the police were absolutely at fault, and then the case was entrusted to Canler, at that time only a chief inspector, but who was to become famous soon as one of the most intelligent heads of the Paris detective force.

The first thing Canler did was to get a description of the pseudo-Mahossier and his accomplice, for he concluded that 'Mahossier' was an alias. The principal tenant of the premises in the Rue Montorgueil was in a position to describe the former, whom he had seen several times, but he knew little or nothing of Mahossier's companion, who had seemingly kept in the dark; Canler's informant had only caught a glimpse of him once. The next step on the detective's part was to impress carefully upon his retina the name of Mahossier as written upon the door of the room. Nowadays the simplest way would be to have the name reproduced by some photographic or other process, but though Daguerre and Niepce de St Victor had begun operations as early as 1829, that kind of science was still in its infancy. Canler, as I have occasion to show—as, in fact, I have already hinted in a previous article — had very advanced notions with regard to the benefits to be derived from publicity of all kinds in the detection of crime. He would certainly not have been guilty of the blunder of the English constable who effaced the supposed handwriting of 'Jack the Ripper' the moment he caught sight of it on the wall in Goulston Street, Whitechapel, lest it should provoke a crowd and a scandal. He would very likely have invited people to impress that handwriting on their memory. This by the way.

Provided with those mental notes, Canler began to make the tour of the *garnis* of the capital. It is rather difficult to convey to the English reader an idea of the *hôtel garni* in the French metropolis and large centres. The London coffee-shop where they let beds is the nearest approach to it, but there are few bachelors or single women in London, however badly off, who have never had any other home since they left their parents' roof. There are thousands of French men and French women engaged in business, and often in remunerative business, who have spent the greater part of their lives in the *hôtel garni*—nay, who have lived in the same one for years. From the highest to the lowest they are all under the strict supervision of the police, and the proprietor or manager thereof is bound to keep a register wherein to inscribe the name of his lodgers; if a private individual sub-lets a furnished room or a set he is bound to do the same, which register is open to the inspection of the police at any hour during the day or night.

The reader must work out the rest for himself, but it will not take him long to see that under such conditions the search for suspicious characters is greatly facilitated. Canler's investigations proved fruitless, though, for nearly two days, and then he came upon the name of 'Mahossier' in the register of a *garni* in the Faubourg du Temple, and underneath that name the one of Ficellier. The two individuals in question had occupied the same bed. The description of Mahossier given by the landlady tallied so exactly with that supplied by Genevey himself and by the principal tenant of the house in the Rue Montorgueil as to make Canler feel confident of being on the track of the two individuals wanted. But he felt puzzled with regard to Ficellier. As the woman proceeded to give his verbal portrait Canler became convinced that he had him under lock and key already, though not under that name. A few days previously a certain François had been arrested on the charge of having obtained several casks of wine by fraud. Full of this new discovery Canler returned to the depôt, where, then as now, every prisoner, is detained until he has undergone a first examination by the *juge d'instruction*, or by one of the substitutes of the Procurator-General.

François was still there, and locked up in a cell—which is rarely the case even now, except with prisoners charged with serious crimes. Canler had himself shown in. I have already alluded to the difference in that respect between English and Continental criminal procedure, so need not enlarge upon it any more. Canler plunged *in medias res* at once, utterly regardless of our axiom about a prisoner incriminating himself, 'I have been puzzling my brain for the last four-and-twenty hours,' he began, ' why you went to Pageot's *garni* under the name of Ficellier, the more that you told me you had had no hand in that affair of the casks of wine.'

François fell into the trap. 'I knew there was a warrant out against me,' he answered, 'and I wasn't idiot enough to give my own name for your agents to lay hands on me.'

Hence there was no doubt about François having stayed in the Faubourg du Temple in company with Mahossier on the night of the attempted murder. The natural surmise was that François was the latter's accomplice. Canler made a report to that effect. Still, there was no other trace of Mahossier, who was evidently the principal offender. As a kind of forlorn hope, Canler returned to the Faubourg du Temple to get some further information from Madame Pageot,,the husband being rather taciturn by nature, and furthermore apparently disinclined in this instance to talk freely about his lodgers. Chance befriended the detective. During a long conversation with the woman he gathered incidentally that Mahossier had stayed in the place before, but under the name of Bâton. The revelation nearly took Canler's breath away. He only knew Bâton by repute, but felt sure he could lay hands on him within a few hours, and, in fact, that same evening Bâton was arrested at a café at the back of the theatre of the Porte St Martin. But Canler felt more puzzled than ever. Bâton's appearance did not tally in the least with the description of Mahossier as given by Genevey and the principal tenant of the house in the Rue Montorgueil. Nor did they recognise Bâton when confronted with him. François up till then had been left in ignorance of the graver charge against him, and now Genevey would not positively swear to him, while Gousseaux's (the tenant's) evidence was even of a more negative kind. The authorities were obliged, therefore to discharge Bâton ; but information had reached the Prefecture of Police meanwhile, that Bâton was on very intimate terms with a certain Gaillard, who had been his fellow-prisoner at Poissy. The very moment of Bâton's discharge Canler met him, casually as it were, at the door of the Prefecture, and accompanied him part of the way. He very discreetly brought the conversation round to Gaillard, and in a little while became convinced that Gaillard and Mahossier were one and the same person. Consequently it was Gaillard that was wanted. There could be no doubt about it this time. Gaillard, therefore, was not only in the habit of assuming aliases, but of choosing by preference the names of some of his comrades. And, as it happened, his own—if Gaillard was his own, which up to that time seemed probable — would have stood him in better stead for throwing people off the scent than either that of Mahossier or Bàton, both of which were far less common. This was proved by Canler having to select from at least a score of Gaillards inscribed on the registers of the *garnis* during the twelvemonth previous to the crime, whereas he had not met with a single Mahossier or Bâton. And still it is no exaggeration to say that Lacenaire was a criminal of genius. It was instinct that finally put Canler on the right scent, but to a greater extent still that much-desired aid to criminal detection on the Continent, the criminal who turns informer. But, as we shall see presently, 'between the scent and the view' the matter was virtually taken out of Canler's hands.

For the present we must accompany
Canler to the end of his two days' search,
when, in a *garni* in the Rue Marivaux-des-
Lombards, he instinctively felt that he had
come upon the track of the right Gaillard.
So sure was he of this that a question which
he had not put previously to any of the
landlords he put there and then ; 'Did this
Gaillard leave no papers or linen or clothing
behind him ?' he asked.

'There was a bundle of Republican ditties
on the shelf of the room he occupied,' was
the answer.

In another moment the detective was
turning over the songs in question, in a
moment after that he came upon an insult-
ing letter addressed to the Prefect of Police,
the handwriting of which, even to his eye,
unskilled in such matters, tallied exactly
with that of Mahossier as displayed on the
door of the room in the Rue Montorgueil.
If there had been a doubt up till then in

Canler's mind as to Mahossier's identity, it was set at rest at once.

That was how things stood when an individual named Avril, who had been sentenced a few days previously to a twelvemonth, sent word to the Prefecture that he would undertake to find Gaillard if they would allow him to roam Paris for a week —of course, in company of a detective. The offer was accepted, but the results were nil. Meanwhile François, who was implicated in the attempted murder of Genevey by his tacit admission of having spent the night of the crime with Mahossier, was being constantly interrogated by the examining magistrate. One day, when escorted by Canler from Sainte-Pelagie to the Palace of Justice, he volunteered information with regard to the murder of a widow Chardon and her son, committed exactly a fortnight before the affair of the Rue Montorgueil, and the perpetrators of which had up till that time baffled all pursuit, seeing that their identity was not so much as surmised by the police.

François professed to have the account of the crime from Gaillard himself, who had confided it to him on New Year's Day, after a lunch that had been prolonged from one P.M. till past midnight. As a matter of course, Canler communicated immediately with his chief, in whose presence François repeated his statement, from which it appeared that Gaillard was also the principal author of that crime. Still there was no trace of Gaillard. At this particular juncture Avril sent a second message to the police to the effect that Gaillard had an aunt living in the Rue Bar-du-Bec, in the house of a packing-case maker. Canler, accompanied by his chief, M. Allard, repaired at once to the indicated address, and found that an old lady of the name of Gaillard, living on her income, occupied a set of rooms on the second floor. Their ring at the bell was answered by the old lady herself, but not in the usual way. Instead of the door being opened, a grizzled head appeared behind a trap in the panel. 'What do you want, gentlemen?' came the question. 'We should like to speak to Madame Gaillard,' was the answer. 'I am Madame Gaillard.' 'We should like to ask you a few questions with regard to your nephew Gaillard.' 'First of all, gentlemen, my nephew's name is Lacenaire, and not Gaillard; he is a thorough bad lot, who means to murder me for my little bit of money if he gets the chance. That's why I have had this trap made in the door, so that I may be able to see people before I let them in; and if ever he calls, I shall take particular good care not to admit him.'

Thus they were really dealing with a human chameleon, who, if he did not change his appearance, changed his name at will. Nor were the surprises at an end, for while Canler was looking for Lacenaire in Paris, news came from the authorities at Beaune that Lacenaire had been apprehended in that city while trying to pass a forged bill of exchange under the name of Levy Jacob.

We may at once state that Lacenaire was tried for, convicted of, and sentenced to death for the murder of the widow Chardon and her son, in which Avril had been his accomplice. The attempt upon the bank porter was not even made a count in the indictment. Our main purpose in this paper has been to sketch Lacenaire, not to give a detailed account of one or two of his crimes. Balzac and Gaboriau, Wilkie Collins and Miss Braddon, who may be taken as the foremost exponents of fiction dealing with crime, have never evolved from their brains any fiend in human shape to compare with him—nay, the annals of crime throughout the world scarcely present his counterpart. Joseph Philippe, though he paid the penalty of his deeds with his life, was virtually a maniac; Heinrich Kempen and Troppmann,

had they escaped after their first exploits,
would probably have stopped at these;
Charles Peace only murdered when necessity—'his necessity'—compelled; Georges
Lacenaire deliberately planned murder, irrespective of the resistance of his victim,
irrespective of the amount to be gained by
it.   Avinain, Prévôt, and Dumollard—
all Frenchmen — were untutored, the first
and last named being scarcely one degree
removed from the brute of the field;
Georges Lacenaire was an educated man,
with a considerable taste for literature and
art, an instinctive turn for poetry, and a
critical faculty which, if utilised, might
have borne good fruit. While still osten-
sibly in the ranks of those who get their
livelihood by honest labour, he was offered
the copying of a three-act comedy.   He
accepted, but forty-eight hours later returned the rough manuscript to the authors,
saying, 'I have read this, but could not
lend myself to copying such drivel, it makes

me positively sick.' Throughout his incarceration he was not only uniformally polite to his gaolers, but most courteous to his visitors. 'And the courteousness,' said M. Allard, 'was not studied for the occasion ; it was the manner of a man gently bred and reared.'

This was the man whom M. Allard and Canler went to see immediately after his arrival in Paris. His hands and feet were manacled, and he was lying on a small camp bedstead in his cell. They spoke to him of the crime of the Rue Montorgueil. He admitted at once that he was one of the authors of it, but without the least bravado or the least regret. He treated the affair as a merchant might treat an unlucky operation. When asked to give the names of his accomplices, he simply replied, 'Gentlemen, our pride lies in never turning round upon our accomplices, unless they themselves peach upon us. So you need not expect any information on that point from me.'

But when Canler showed him conclusively that not only François but Avril had 'blown the gaff' in connection with the murder of the widow Chardon, that the former had narrated the whole of the story as told to him by Lacenaire, and that the other had perambulated Paris for a week in company with Canler, trying to find him, and had furthermore indicated the domicile of Lacenaire's aunt, he promised to verify the statement, and, in the event of its proving true, to speak out. He kept his word, and confessed everything. His conclusion was characteristic. 'I know,' he said, 'that for the affair in the Rue Montorgueil I should have been sentenced to penal servitude for life only, while for the affair Chardon I shall be executed, but it does not matter — it is the only way of being revenged on Avril and François, who have so basely betrayed me.' After his sentence, and contrary to the usual custom, Lacenaire was allowed to remain at the

Conciergerie instead of being transferred to either Bicêtre or La Force, La Roquette not being thought of at that time. For the benefit of my readers, I may tell them that the Conciergerie, notwithstanding the burning of the Palace of Justice by the Communists, still remains. It forms the north-eastern angle of the new structure, and may be recognised from the outside by the turret surmounting it.

To return to Lacenaire. The authorities felt they were dealing with no ordinary criminal. During the previous four years numberless crimes had been committed, the authors of which had remained undetected. It was surmised, rightly or wrongly, that Lacenaire had had a hand in them ; and the authorities hoped, by their lenient treatment of him—under the circumstances—to induce him to speak. They were doomed to disappointment, albeit that, up till a few hours before his death, they clung to the hope. Lacenaire opposed a steadfast refusal to every attempt at making him betray the comrades who had remained true to him. He was as courteous, as polite as ever, but nothing Canler could say made him depart from his resolution. Canler himself has frankly admitted the superiority of the man, the charm of his conversation, his great intelligence. 'And still,' he remarked one day to Lacenaire—'and still in the Rue Montorgueil affair you seem to have utterly departed from your usual caution?'

'That is true,' answered Lacenaire, 'but not in the way you mean. Let me hear your notion of where I was at fault, and I will tell you mine afterwards.'

'If you had succeeded in killing Genevey, you would have got away with the money and the notes, but the body would have remained behind, and the only difference would have been that we should have found a dead man, instead of a seriously wounded one. It would have made no difference to the police, because Messieurs Maigre-

Morstadt and Mallet would have supplied
the needed first clue, and I should have
found out that Mahossier, Bâton, Gaillard,
and Lacenaire were one and the same.'

'That's where you are mistaken. When
I organised one of those affairs, I always
took care to foresee the results, and to prevent the consequences. You know that
there were two trusses of straw in the room.
If I had killed Genevey, I should have cut
him up, and, by means of the straw, and a
large piece of oilcloth which I had upon me,
packed him in the basket. After that I
should have taken a small house half-a-
dozen miles away from Paris, and boiled
down the separate parts of the body for the
space of twenty-four hours. An enormous
fire would have done the rest for the bones,
and there would have been no difficulty in
disposing of the ashes. Now, do you perceive that I might easily have defied all the
detectives in the world, yourself included,
to find the slightest trace of the crime?

True, there would have been the disappearance of Genevey to account for, but do you know what would have been the result of that? No? Well, I will tell you. Instigated by public imbecility, which professes to think no evil and which never does anything else, you would have raised the hue and cry after Genevey, whom you and all the rest would have suspected of having absconded with the money. I will tell you Monsieur Canler, where I departed from my usual caution, and well I know it, for I shall pay for it with my head. I departed from my usual caution by taking a partner in this as well as in the Chardon affair. But for them, I should by now be in America with ten or eleven thousand francs, which would have kept me from want for a couple of years. As you were good enough to say, I am intelligent. My intelligence might have made a merchant prince or a great journalist of me, because I have had a very good education. On the other hand, if I had worked alone no one could have split upon me; I should not have been obliged to split upon others, etc., etc. I am the more sorry for this, seeing that these were the only times, except once, that I availed myself of aid, without which I should always have done better, because the failure of the Genevey affair is entirely due to the cowardice of François, who ran away the moment the fellow began to cry out. Wherever I have acted alone no one has been any the wiser, whether in small or great things.'

'How do you know? We may be in possession of facts we did not care to publish.'

'I do know. But as I was absolutely alone in these things, I may tell you some of them. They implicate no one, and the law cannot cut off my head twice.

'You are aware that I belong to Lyons, where my father was a well-to-do trader, who became a bankrupt through his generosity to, and confidence in, others rather than through his own fault. But, though we were by no means rich after that, there was no necessity for me to rob or to kill. I do not wish to make myself out better or worse than I am, consequently I am not going to tell you that I deliberately planned my first theft or murder, nor am I going to say that I felt the slightest remorse afterwards. On the night I robbed and drowned my first victim I slept as soundly as ever, and I do not think that from that night until this moment I have given the stranger a single thought.

'It happened in this way. I was returning home from a 'spree' with some of my comrades one summer's morning just before daybreak. They left me before we crossed the Morand Bridge. About half-way on it I met with a gentleman who had evidently been dining too well, for he was rather unsteady in his walk. Just in the flicker of the street lamp I noticed that he had a magni-

ficent gold chain.   He was very well dressed;
so without a moment's hesitation I made
sure that no one was in sight, then caught
him by the throat, throttled him, and robbed
him of everything he had upon him—his
chain, his watch, and his pocketbook, which,
by-the-bye, contained five thousand francs
in notes.   I might have left him there, for,
though almost suffocated, he was not dead,
but I thought it better to get rid of him
altogether, so I took him round the waist,
and, though he was by no means light, I
managed to hoist him on to the parapet,
whence I pushed him into the Rhône.   I
never knew who he was, for I had operated
by myself, and felt certain that I was safe.
At present I should probably read the papers
and watch for the account of his disappearance.   At that time I did not even trouble
myself, but I took care not to part with the
watch and chain until I got to Paris some
time afterwards.'

'Do you know,' he said on another occasion, ' how I got my living when first I came to Paris? I do not mean the miserable pittance I earned as a copying clerk, I mean the living when I was supposed to be a young fellow of means. You do not? Well, I got it by the *vol à la cire*. Ruolz, Christofle, and all the rest of the electro-platers have to thank me for part of their success, because during two years I ab-stracted no less than twelve hundred silver spoons and as many silver forks from the different restaurants in Paris. It was I who invented the process of sticking a spoon and a fork underneath the table by means of cobblers' wax, and taking them away after I had paid my bill, when the waiter had cleared the table without missing them. In an evil hour, when I became somewhat spotted, I took a partner; it was he who landed us in Poissy. While I worked alone I had many a queer escape, but there was never a fork or spoon found upon me. I used to leave the restaurant apparently very indignant when such a charge was brought, because the proprietor was perforce obliged to apologise when he found the missing articles on the floor. I never took more than one fork and one spoon at a time. My partner was not satisfied with such small gains, and must needs take three or four at once. It ought to have taught me a lesson; but, you see, it did not.

'When I came out of Poissy, I had a bit of money. Almost immediately after my return to Paris I went to a gaming-house in the Palais Royal to try my luck. In less than a quarter of an hour I was cleaned out. Next to me sat a young fellow who apparently had an extraordinary run of luck, for at ten o'clock he was about ten thousand francs to the good. When I saw him get up to go, the idea suddenly struck me to go after him, kill him, and get hold of his money; but a second thought convinced me that the hour was badly chosen. It was only ten o'clock, consequently too early to attempt such a thing in the streets of Paris. I made up my mind to watch for a better opportunity, but, though I watched for a week, no better opportunity came.   But on the ninth night, about twelve o'clock, a gentleman came who in less than an hour won thirty thousand francs, put them in his pocketbook, and left without saying a word. There was the chance I had been waiting for, I followed him, and when we got to the Rue Blanche in a very dark spot, I came suddenly upon him with uplifted dagger and threatened to kill him if he uttered a syllable. He was more dead than alive already with fear, and about to hand me over the money, when in the distance we heard the steady tramp of the patrol.   Thereupon my man began to shout with all his might, and I was obliged to take to my heels.   I told you before that whenever I planned a thing the 'quieting' of my victim was the first part of the proceedings.   If I had adhered to my original method that night, instead of parleying, I should have had the money, because he would not have uttered a sound ; and I should have had time to rifle his pockets, seeing that the patrol was quite at the other end of the street. That taught me another lesson.'

I cannot report in full the whole of Lacenaire's conversation, nor any of his poetry, which has the pessimistic but true ring about it. He was executed on the same morning with his accomplice Avril, and, notwithstanding the official account to the contrary, died game. His pessimism, his avowed hostility to society, his atheism, had caused a great noise. The authorities were bent upon proving that at the last moment he became a coward, and chance befriended them. The *Gazette des Tribunaux* had sent a reporter who, being a stranger to the staff and to the military, failed to elbow his way through. He went to the Prefecture for the account of the execution, and they supplied it as they wished it set forth. But

Canler, who was by Lacenaire's side up to the end, declared the account to be entirely false. In fact, that great detective says that Lacenaire died as he had lived, utterly regardless of the value of human life, and that 'nothing in his life became him like the leaving it.'

THE SECRET OF THE GUILLOTINE

About seven o'clock in the evening of June 5, 1864, M. Beauquesne, the governor of La Roquette, was told by his servant that a visitor wished to speak to him. The latter was no less a personage than the celebrated Alfred Louis Velpeau, the greatest French surgeon of his time, who came provided with an order to see a colleague, Dr Edmond de la Pommeraies, lying under sentence of death. In silence the two men proceeded to the 'condemned cell;' there was a rattling of muskets on the flags of the corridor, the door was opened; at a sign of the governor, the warder and the

soldier on guard retired, almost immediately
followed by M. Beauquesne himself, and the
visitor and his host were left alone.

It would be difficult to find a greater
contrast than that existing between the two
men. Velpeau, the world-renowned savant,
the son of an obscure provincial farrier, was
then in his sixtieth year. The rugged
though kindly face, the grey hair, the un-
pretending dress might have been those of
the merest commonplace tradesman. It was
only when he spoke that one felt to be in the
presence of a genius; it was only when his
deep-set eyes lighted up that one felt confronted by the bold inquirer who dragged
the secrets from nature herself for the benefit
of suffering humanity. According to all
those who knew him, no such comforting
impression could be derived from a glance at
de la Pommeraies. Though young and
exceedingly handsome, men fought instinctively shy of him; on the other hand, he was
a great favourite with many members of the

fair sex. His professional brethren did not deny him a certain amount of talent, but they averred that it was by no means in proportion to his pretensions. His social attainments, not his medical capacities, had gained him the position he occupied. It was by means of the former that he had succeeded in contracting an advantageous marriage with Mdlle. Dubizy, a charming girl, highly accomplished, the daughter of a wealthy physician, notwithstanding the opposition of the latter's widow. Madame Dubizy had never any faith in her intended son-in-law, and her daughter's marriage settlement attested this suspicion on her part. The dowry (£6,000, a considerable one even in those days) was strictly tied up. Consequently, from a financial point of view, de la Pommeraies was as little advanced as ever, and compelled to continue his stock exchange speculations, his dabbling in shady and bogus companies, which had already damaged both his credit and his reputation. Two months after the union, Madame Dubizy who up till then had been in excellent health, is taken with violent vomiting after a dinner party at de la Pommeraies', and though two different doctors are called in their prescriptions are not even made up.   Her son-in-law himself attends on her, with the result that she expires next morning, 'carried off by an attack of cholera,' to borrow de la Pommeraies' own words.   Thereupon de la Pommeraies lays hands on all his mother-in-law's personal property, amounting to £2000, refusing to give the slightest account of it, claiming its absolute possession in the name of his wife, the only child and sole heiress, seeing that no will is found.

Curiously enough, though rumours of foul play were rife, though the man's record at the Prefecture of Police was not a clean one, he was not molested.   The authorities shirked the responsibility of arresting a physician in professedly good practice, and, moreover, moving in good society.   We

must remember that in the hey-day of the
Second Empire 'good society' was a somewhat elastic term, because it would have
been a difficult matter to determine the
precise point at which it merged into the
reverse.

For the next two years de la Pommeraies
tries to improve his social and professional
position, not by the legitimate exercise of
his profession, but by profuse expenditure,
by giving showy entertainments, etc., etc.
As a matter of course his means cannot bear
this strain, and, by the provisions of his
marriage settlement, he cannot convert his
wife's property into ready money; he can
only enjoy the interest thereof. She herself
cannot help him further than this, the
property being vested in trustees. Nor, as
it transpired subsequently, would her death
have benefited him; but we may charitably
infer that, even had this not been the case,
her life would still have been sacred to him.
For it is but fair to state that this heartless

adventurer, this calculating Don Juan, who had hitherto made woman his stepping stone, sincerely loved his wife, loved her to a degree such as to have ceased all intercourse with his former mistress before his wedding-day, to have refused all communication with her, notwithstanding her repeated requests, to have declined attending her children during their illness, lest the contact with the mother should shake his resolution. English readers who have not studied the complications of French married life arising from ante-nuptial relations may deem it surprising that we should have mentioned this; those who know something of the undercurrents of French matrimony will not deem our praise uncalled for.

To resume. De la Pommeraies, then, though exceedingly happy in his home life, was sorely pressed for money. It will always remain a matter of more or less conjecture how he would have faced his difficulties, whether during these two years he was looking out for a new victim ; but one thing is certain, that but for one circumstance the victim eventually selected would never have been thought of. My conviction to that effect is a purely moral one ; it is not based upon anything that transpired at the trial, nor have I ever met with a confirmation of my view in any account of the proceedings; still, I am positive that it is not a mere theory on my part.

I happened to be frequently in Paris between the years 1859 and 1864, and I distinctly remember the publication of a French version of an English book dealing with celebrated criminal trials. I have often tried to find the work, but I had nothing to guide me in my search, not even the title or the name of the author. I was very young at the time I read it, and it was long afterwards that the thought struck me to read it a second time. This much I do recollect; the volume contained a narrative of the trial of Palmer, the Rugeley murderer, and of another doctor who was arraigned for having killed, by means of digitaline, the woman he had bigamously married. She had made a will in his favour. He was acquitted, either for want of sufficient evidence, or because that evidence, from the medical point of view, was too conflicting, and afterwards tried for bigamy. He was sentenced to twelve months' imprisonment, at the expiration of which he successfully defended the validity of the will against her relations. More than this I do not know, but I repeat I am certain that the book must have fallen into de la Pommeraies' hands, and suggested to him the plan of his subsequent crime, though it differed considerably from the original. The reader may judge for himself. In 1861 de la Pommeraies ceased all intercourse with Madame de Pauw, who had then been his mistress for more than three years. In June, 1863, he paid her an unsolicited visit, and, to explain this sudden change in his sentiments, he pretended to be concerned for the lot of her children. Beyond telling her that he intends to insure her life he enters into no particulars that day; still, he recommends the greatest secrecy. Their relations having been resumed, de la Pommeraies unfolds his scheme more fully. He is going to insure her life in several offices for the amount of £20,000, the premiums will be paid by him, the policies are to be made out in his favour. In reply to Madame de Pauw's question how this transaction can possibly benefit her children, he submits the following combination: When the affair has been concluded Madame de Pauw is to sham a very severe illness, which will lead the companies to believe that her life is in danger. As a matter of course they will become alarmed at the prospect of having to pay so vast a sum, and then de la Pommeraies will go and see them in her name, and propose a compromise. The policies will be cancelled in consideration of an annuity of £220 during Madame de Pauw's life. As she will be apparently at the point of death, the companies will only be too glad to be let off so cheaply. Thanks to this stratagem she and her children will be provided for life. Without considering for a moment the fraudulent nature of such a transaction, and swayed above all by her renewed passion for her lover, in whom, moreover, she sees the guardian angel of her children, Madame de Pauw consents. She does not for a moment suspect the real drift of his machinations, although one of the conditions imposed by him ought at any rate to have opened her eyes to his financial straits and made her wonder whence he was to get the necessary funds to pay the important premiums. For he stipulated that half of the annual income should go to him. But love is often worse than blind, it is defective of vision, and knows it not. The blind are on their guard, and only on an emergency trust to their instinct, which seldom leads them wrong, the unconsciously short sighted rush on, mistaking the *cul-de-sac* for the short cut.

Though de la Pommeraies wished to direct the operations, he was too cautious to appear in the affair, which was throughout negotiated by an insurance agent named Desmidt whose reputation, as it subsequently transpired, was by no means spotless. Eight different policies, amounting in all to 550,000 francs, were issued by eight different companies in favour of Madame de Pauw, whose health, as attested by the physicians attached to these offices, left nothing to desire. Though the premiums, amounting to close upon 19,000 francs were paid by Madame de Pauw herself, no secret was made of the funds having been furnished by the Comte de la Pommeraies (who was no more a count than I am) in order to provide for the children of the insured lady, of whom he was alleged to be the father—another falsehood, which was not revealed till afterwards. The insurances were effected for the benefit of the children. Each policy might be transferred to a third person by a simple endorsement; but notice had to be given to that effect to the office of issue. To make assurance doubly sure, de la Pommeraies began by having each of these policies endorsed in his favour by Madame de Pauw in consideration of the receipts for the premiums held by him. He furthermore made her execute a will by which she acknowledged to be indebted to him for 550,000 francs—in short he took every possible precaution to have no litigation at her demise.

And the demise followed hard upon the termination of all these contracts. Towards the end of September she began to complain to her friends of having had a serious fall down the staircase, and of feeling very unwell indeed. She consulted several doctors, who prescribed for her. This was altogether in accordance with the plan agreed upon between them, but de la Pommeraies committed a terrible blunder in not having had the perscriptions made up. Nor did Madame de Pauw cease to attend to her ordinary occupations until the beginning of November, when, at the recommendation of her lover, and ' in order to hoodwink more effectually the physicians of the insurance companies deputed to call upon her,' as he said, she took to her bed. Not content with this, de la Pommeraies made her take a draught which, according to him, would produce an appearance of feverishness. Unfortunately, Madame de Pauw had, notwithstanding the express recommendation of de la Pommeraies, confided the particulars of the conspiracy to a friend, Mdlle. Hullmand, to whom she constantly repeated that in a short time she would be comfortable for the remainder of her life, alluding to the expected annuity of 3,000fr. On November 13, she writes to another friend, Madame Ridder, to come and spend the evening with her, and she discusses her happy prospects in equally sanguine terms. Meanwhile there is not the slightest indication of the visit of the physicians. She grows really very ill, though she tries to make light of it to her daughters. De la Pommeraies arrives at the same time on the spot, and states that Madame de Pauw is suffering from an attack of cholerine, but that she will be all right in a day or two. In a day or two she is a corpse. In the evening of November 16 she breathes her last, attended by Mdlle. Hullmand, who on going down-stairs to inform the *concierge*, meets de la Pommeraies, to whom she conveys the sad news, at which he seems neither shocked nor surprised. 'It is as I expected,' he says, standing by the bedside ; 'the conse-quences of the fall have killed her.' There-upon Mdlle. Hullmand tells him plainly that he is stating a lie, that her friend never had a fall, and informs him that the deceased woman has told her everything.

The first rumbling of the storm about to
burst over his head ought to have warned
de la Pommeraies not to be rash, but in so
evident a hurry is he to get possession of the
insurance moneys that he throws all precaution to the winds and applies to the companies on the very morrow of Madame de
Pauw's death, when her body is scarcely
cold.   And though in this, as in the former
instance, there are loud whispers that all is
not right, though an information is laid
against him by the deceased's brother-in-law,
M. Gouchon, the authorities are reluctant
to move.   Madame de Pauw is buried,
several weeks elapse, the companies are
about to settle the claim, and de la
Pommeraies may well flatter himself that
the earth covers all traces of his second
crime.

But M. Gouchon sticks to his text that
Madame de Pauw has been foully done away
with, and at last the police consent to the
exhumation of the body and its examination

by Professor Tardieu, both of which are performed in the middle of the night. M. de Gonet, of whom I have spoken in connection with Philippe, is entrusted with the affair, but he also hesitates, considering that the eminent savant finds no traces of foul play. The intestines have not been tampered with. What is to be done? Things would come to a pretty pass if on a mere suspicion the police were to arrest people, and especially doctors. The whole of the corporation would revolt. Moreover, M. de Gonet is morally convinced of de la Pommeraies' innocence. Still, he does not think himself justified in giving him a chance to escape, in the event of his being guilty, which assuredly he would endeavour to do at the first rumour of what had taken place in the dissecting-room of Professor Tardieu.

Consequently, early one morning at the end of December he presents himself at de la Pommeraies' residence before the doctor is fairly out of bed, and is received

in the most charming manner. The physician does not evince the slightest sign of
emotion, and during an hour's friendly chat
remains cool and collected, professing his
willingness to afford the police every information with regard to his relations with
Madame de Pauw.   Saying which, he
opens a drawer of his writing table and
takes from it a bundle of letters carefully tied
with a ribbon.   'These are her letters,' he
concludes , 'read, and judge for yourself.'
The sight of these letters acts like a flash
of lightning on M. de Gonet's brain.   They
are the defence prepared by a guilty man
who is hourly expecting a visit from the
police.   This keen and experienced magistrate has no longer a doubt with regard to
de la Pommeraies' crime.   But M. de
Gonet's face betrays no sign of suspicion.
He continues to chat.   'I was perfectly
convinced of all this before I called,' he says
in his usual tone.   'Still, there are certain
formalities to be gone through; an official

report of our conversation to be drawn up. Would it not be better to go to my room at the Palais de Justice instead of remaining here, where we may be disturbed at any moment by one of your numerous patients? Can you spare me half-an-hour?'

'Certainly,' replies de la Pommeraies in the same cheerful tone.

The interview between the examining magistrate and de la Pommeraies in the former's room lasted for ten hours, at the end of which the physician was conveyed to Mazas, formally charged with the murder of Madame de Pauw.

We need not follow the trial step by step. In spite of the masterly defence of Maître Lachaud; in spite of the eminent experts called by the latter, the circumstantial evidence against de la Pommeraies was too crushing, and on the 17th May, 1864, he was sentenced to death on the unanimous verdict of the jury. (In France a majority is sufficient to legalise a verdict.)

This was the man who, on Alfred Velpeau entering his cell, had risen from his seat, and stood looking at the eminent surgeon for a few moments, after which he beckoned him to the chair he had just vacated. he himself leaning against his bed and waiting in silence for his visitor to speak.

'Monsieur,' began the latter at last, 'between doctors there is little need of ceremony in discussing death. I myself belong to the category of the condemned.'

'Then, according to you, monsieur, I have no hope left,' interrupted de la Pommeraies.

'I am afraid not, but you have at any rate a few days before you. Besides, my proposal is conditional. If your life be spared, so much the better; if not—'

'If not?' repeated de la Pommeraies.

Instead of answering directly, Velpeau took from his pocket a small case of surgical instruments, and with a lancet slit the sleeve of de la Pommeraies' strait-jacket; then placed his finger on his pulse.

'Your pulse,' he said, 'shows a firmness, a perfectly composed state which, under the circumstances, is rare indeed; consequently I will go straight to the point. You are aware that one of the most interesting problems of modern physiology is to find out whether a flash or a gleam of real memory, of reflection, of feeling, remains in the human brain after the severance of the head from the trunk.'

'I am aware of it,' replied his interlocutor. 'I am acquainted with all that has been said and written on the subject. I was even present at one of your lectures on the subject, and I am afraid to say that I do not quite agree with your conclusions. Theoretically I believe that such a gleam remains. In less than a week I shall know for certain, but alas, I shall also have forgotten.'

'You will have forgotten, but before then

you may have enlightened humanity and science for ever,' slowly said Velpeau keeping his eyes fixed on de la Pommeraies. Then, all of a sudden—'And to beat about the bush no longer, this is what I have come for. I have been deputed by a committee of our most eminent colleagues in Paris, and here is my pass, signed by the Emperor himself. It confers upon me the power even of postponing your execution if necessary.'

' I do not quite understand,' said the condemned man, looking blankly at his visitor.

' Let me explain, then, M. de la Pommeraies. In the name of that science which, whatever may happen individually to one of her students, is always dear to us—in the name of that science which counts her hundreds of martyrs among those who laboured to master her secrets—I have come to claim from you an example of courage and energy greater than that ever claimed from any human being, provided an experiment, agreed between us, be feasible, which I doubt. If your petition be rejected, you, of all others, are the most competent subject upon whom to demonstrate an attempt at communication. I do not overlook—provided, I repeat, that such communication be possible—the difficulties of the attempt even with you ; but, if after the execution you could convey a sign of intelligence, your service to science would render for ever illustrious your name. The scientific glory attached to it would more than efface the social stigma.'

'I begin to understand,' whispered de la Pommeraies, who had turned ghastly white.

'I need not assure you that your remains will be laid to rest immediately after the event, without one of our scalpels touching you. I shall be facing you when the knife drops ; your head will pass as quickly as possible from the hands of the executioner into mine. And then — seeing that the experiment can only be conclusive in proportion to its being simplified.—I will whisper very distinctly into your ear: " Monsieur Couty de la Pommeraies, in remembrance of our agreement, can you *at this moment* lower your right eyelid three times in succession, while keeping the other eye wide open?" If *at that moment*, whatever may be the other facial contractions, you can show me by this triple movement that you have understood, that by an act of permanent will, you have overcome all the horror, all the crowding impressions of your sinking consciousness,—if you can do this, the fact will be sufficent to enlighten science, to revolutionise our convictions. And be sure, monsieur, that I shall notify the fact in such a manner as to invest your memory with the halo of a hero rather than with the stigma of a criminal.'

When Velpeau ceased speaking, de la Pommeraies sat for a few moments, as if petrified ; then he answered : ' The violence of the blow may, notwithstanding all my efforts, prevent me from remembering all this at the moment of death. Besides, the chances of remaining vitality may not be the same in all those who are decapitated. Nevertheless, monsieur, come back on the morning of the execution. I will then give you my answer.'

A moment afterwards Velpeau had left the cell.

* * * * *

For nearly seventy-two hours after this interview it seemed doubtful whether the experiment agreed upon between the two physicians would have a chance of being carried out. In the afternoon of June 8, Maître Lachaud took the unhappy wife of the condemned man to the Tuileries, where he had been granted an interview with the Empress. The latter promised to intercede with the Emperor, who there and then pledged himself to spare de la Pommeraies' life. Madame de la Pommeraies jumped into a cab, and wrote a few words in pencil to her husband—'The Emperor will commute your sentence.'

Three hours later a Cabinet Council was held at the Tuileries, and Napoleon, faithful to his word, proposed to commute the sentence. The whole body of Ministers opposed the step. De la Pommeraies' profession, which had made the authorities reluctant to move in the case of Madame Dubizy, now became the alleged reason for the law being allowed to take its course. The condemned man belonged to a corporation which held the lives of the public in their very hands; an example was imperatively necessary, etc. The Emperor submitted to his Ministers; orders were given for the execution to take place next morning. Neither the Empress nor Madame de la Pommeraies was informed of the decision, but the eminent barrister went to La Roquette and acquainted the condemned man with what had taken place. He did not wish him to think during his last moments that his wife had purposely deceived him.

*　　*　　*　　*　　*

The morning of the 9th June broke gloriously, and at five o'clock the condemned man was awakened. Among those who entered his cell was Velpeau. After ten minutes' conversation with the Abbé Crouzès, he turned to the eminent surgeon. 'I have practised,' he said; and while the death-warrant was read to him he closed his right eye, while he kept the left wide open.

A quarter of an hour afterwards the doors of the prison swung on their hinges, and de la Pommeraies stood on the threshold. The fresh morning breeze fanned his forehead, and as he looked up he caught sight of the gleaming steel flashing in the bright sunlight. In three seconds from then there was a horrible thud, and scarcely had its sound died away when the crowd beheld a man stoop over the basket and hold up the gory head. Then he bent still closer to it, and seemed to whisper something in its ear. The crowd stood awestruck, but not for long. Quietly, and with reluctance, as it were, the head was deposited once more in the basket, and the man tucked up his sleeves and washed the blood off his hands in the pail of water, standing ready for the use of the executioner and his assistants.

Subjoined is Velpeau's account of the horrible moment in almost his own words.

'At the first sound of my words the right eyelid drooped, the left eye remaining wide open. 'In the name of your Maker, give me the sign twice more,' I whispered, loud enough to be heard a few yards distant. The eyelid quivered, there was an almost imperceptible movement of the lashes, but it was not raised again. The face became gradually more rigid, and absolutely motionless within five seconds.'

'I myself belong to the category of the

condemned,' Velpeau had said. Within three years of that memorable morning he died, without having solved 'the secret of the guillotine.'

IN LOVE'S DISGUISE

Shortly after nine on Saturday morning, January 7, 1882, Monsieur Guillaume Bernays, a barrister in good practice in Antwerp, left his residence, telling one of his servants that he was going to Brussels on business, and that he would be back at six, in time for dinner. The message, left with a mere servant, affords a pertinent insight into the conjugal relations of Monsieur and Madame Bernays. Theirs was, in fact, a house divided against itself. The marriage, which dated from the year 1873, had not been a happy one. There were, no doubt, faults on both sides; still, it would appear that the husband was not a sympathetic character, that he had made few friends, while the wife was universally described as being of a charming disposition, exceedingly charitable and accomplished, though somewhat inclined to take a too romantic and idealistic view of life. Bernays was hard, matter-of-fact, ambitious to a degree, but without the least touch of nobility in that ambition, the wish for emoluments being its mainspring. Dissensions had arisen almost immediately after the union, and with the birth of their first child, a boy, cohabitation had virtually ceased. But for the child, of whom both parents were very fond, divorce would have been resorted to long before the opening of my story, although neither of the parties attempted to charge one another with any of the offences for which a divorce is usually granted in England. The husband had not been guilty of cruelty, the wife at that time had not broken the seventh commandment—whatever she may have done subsequently. It should, however, be remembered that wherever, on the Continent, the law of divorce is in force, a marriage may be dissolved for incompatibility of temper, and of this, at any rate, there was sufficient proof. Monsieur and Madame Bernays had not availed themselves of it, preferring to make for themselves 'a hell in heaven's despite,' as William Blake says. Perhaps not for very long. The painter-poet also speaks of building 'a heaven in hell's despair,' and this Monsieur and Madame Bernays had endeavoured to do in their own way, shortly after the first idea of a divorce had been set aside. Bernays had conceived an intense passion for a handsome maid-servant of his, which if we are to credit subsequent revelations, never exceeded the bounds of platonism; his wife had conceived an equally platonic attachment, 'only more so,' for a gentleman named Armand Peltzer. It is a very odd, but nevertheless stubborn, fact that these kind of attachments should often begin with a quotation from the Greek philosopher, an invisible angel playing the accompaniment to it on a celestial harp, and wind up with a citation from the Criminal Code, a very visible policeman rattling the handcuffs in the guise of orchestration.

Armand Peltzer belonged to a family in which commercial talents of a very high order seemed to have been sown broadcast. Though of German origin, they had been educated at Verviers and Liège, where most of Armand's brothers and sisters were born. They had afterwards removed to Antwerp, where two of his younger brothers established themselves in business, which, from being exceedingly prosperous at the outset, declined in a couple of years to such an extent that a petition in bankruptcy had to be filed. At that moment Armand, who was a civil engineer by profession, was residing at Buenos Ayres, but at the news of the calamity he hastened home, and was barely in time to have the petition annulled by the sacrifice of all his available property, and by contracting engagements which would leave him financially crippled for many years to come. It was this act of generous duty that first attracted Madame Bernays, whose husband was acting for the brothers of Armand; but her family and that of the Peltzers appear to have been on friendly terms before her marriage. For, curious to relate, the matter-of-fact, prosaic lawyer was deeply impressed by the magnitude of Armand Peltzer's devotion to his brother's interests; he seemed to be never weary of extolling it, and he who had made few friends indeed, who apparently was utterly indifferent to the delights of fellowship, began to cling to Armand Peltzer as Jonathan is said to have clung to David. As a matter of course, Armand Peltzer became a constant visitor at Bernays's home. He was a widower with a little daughter, upon whom he doted: the recollection of his wife's endearing qualities never failed to bring tears to his eyes; he was, moreover, in great difficulties through no fault of his own. Madame Bernays was sympathetic, not to say sentimental, and both her sympathy and sentiment were lost upon her husband. 'What one man neglects, another picks up,' says Byron. Hence, it is not very wonderful that Armand Peltzer and Madame Bernays grew to love one another. We will not determine the exact nature of the relations that existed between them; but it is certain that, rightly or wrongly, Bernays's suspicions had been aroused by means of anonymous letters, servants' gossip, and so forth, and that at the end of September, 1881, Armand Peltzer, who had hitherto enacted the part of conciliator between the wife and the husband in their frequent disagreements, was finally forbidden the house, although Bernays retracted the charges he had made against him and his wife—charges which, if unfounded, as both Armand Peltzer and

Madame Bernays alleged them to be, would have justified an application on the latter's part for a divorce. Her parents and friends eagerly counselled the step, but she again refused, probably from motives similar to those which had prompted her the first time —the prospects of the child, who by then had grown into a handsome, clever boy between eight and nine years old. Still, the conditions of Monsieur and Madame Bernays's married life underwent no improvement; they only met at meals, and Madame, strong, in the consciousness of her innocence, was as friendly as ever with Armand Peltzer when chance threw him in her way at her father's home or when, during Peltzer's daughter's holidays, she looked after the little girl's bodily and mental welfare. In short, the atmosphere of the Bernays's household was that of mutual apathy, whence often spring more terrible tragedies than from downright antipathy That was why Guillaume Bernays, instead of stating his intentions with regard to his return from Brussels to the mistress of the house, had left a message with a mere servant.

*   *   *   *   *

Six o'clock came but not Guillaume Bernays. Nor did he appear that night, nor the following—in fact, he had mysteriously vanished, and for the next ten days all trace of him was lost. The search for him on the part of his wife and her friends does not seem to have been very active, but this indifference was probably and mainly due to two justifiable causes. First of all, Madame Bernays's telegrams to her father-in-law in Brussels on the first night of her husband's disappearance had remained unanswered, and when she presented herself there on the Sunday morning the door was almost shut in her face. Monsieur Bernays senior was of the Jewish persuasion; Madame Bernays junior belonged to the Catholic faith. It is more than probable that the old gentleman disapproved of his son's marriage with a Christian girl, but no evidence to that effect transpired at the subsequent trial. When, however, his son, almost immediately after his union, embraced the Catholic faith himself, he naturally attributed the latter's conversion to the influence of the wife, and felt wroth accordingly. Nothing, however, was further from the truth. Guillaume Bernays's conversion was due to the same kind of cool calculation that had made him propose for the hand of Mademoiselle Julie Pecher, and his wife had not only not prompted him, but had viewed the thing with great contempt. Nevertheless, she and her husband's family had remained estranged, and when the blow fell she was plainly shown the uselessness of counting upon their aid in the search for her missing husband. Secondly, Madame Bernays was not at all certain that evil had befallen her spouse. For some months previously he had talked of retiring from the world, of spending the remainder of his days in a monastery, and though the priest who had baptised and admitted him to the Catholic Church denied all knowledge of his whereabouts by telegraph from Paris, it was surmised that he might have joined a brotherhood elsewhere. From the subsequent proceedings it was evident that no fear of his death was seriously entertained by Madame Bernays, and, as I have already said, the search was not very active.

That is how things stood when on January 18 a letter bearing the Basle postmark and purporting to have been written by one Henry Vaughan two days previously, reached Antwerp. It was addressed ' to the coroner,' though no such official exists in Belgium. The writer began by expressing his horror at having seen in the Belgian papers the inquiries as to the whereabouts of Monsieur Guillaume Bernays, and went on to state that he himself had written two letters ' to the Brussels coroner,' to enlighten that official on the subject. The first of these two had been left on his table at 159 Rue de la Loi in Brussels, in his consternation at the accident that had occurred there on January 7 ; nor did the second—posted when he discovered his oversight—seem to have reached its destination ; 'hence the accident has remained unknown and a new calamity has been added to the first.' Then Henry Vaughan described the accident. 'Monsieur Bernays came to see me by appointment. While we were talking business he caught sight of a pistol, and on my showing it to him, and as I was fidgeting with the trigger to put it right again, while his back was turned, the weapon suddenly went off. Monsieur Bernays dropped to the ground, and I thought he was only wounded ; but when I came back with a basin of water and some ammonia, the blood was flowing from his nose, and I found out, alas ! that he was dead—killed by my hand. My first impulse was to send immediately for the coroner, but

in my despair I reflected upon my friendless position in Brussels. I thought of my wife and child, both very ill, who were expecting my return to them at every moment, and I yielded to the temptation of first taking them to the South, of first seeing my friends, and of informing them of the terrible events that will affect the whole of our future.' There was a great deal more in the same quasi-excited strain, and the letter wound up by saying that the writer would soon give himself up to the authorities in order to court the fullest inquiry.

In consequence of this communication the King's Procurator, accompanied by several detectives and an investigating magistrate, proceeded to the house named in Henry Vaughan's letter. The house was absolutely deserted and but partly furnished ; the blinds were drawn down to their fullest extent, and in the back room on the ground floor they found huddled up in an easy-chair the lifeless body of Guillaume Bernays with a bullet wound in the nape of his neck, which, according to the medical experts, must have caused instantaneous death. There were but few traces of blood on the dead man's clothes, but there was a large patch of blood on the carpet in front of the chair, and in the middle of it what they (the experts) conceived to be the impression of a man's boot, which impression, according to some of them, had been made while the blood was already in a state of coagulation, consequently several hours after Bernays's death; and from all this they concluded that one part of the story as given by Henry Vaughan was false, and that the body must have been lifted into the chair much later than was stated in the communication. But who and what was Henry Vaughan? Was he one of Monsieur Bernays's usual clients? Was he, notwithstanding his foreign name, a Belgian; had anyone ever heard of him before? Was it, in fact, the man's real name? To all these questions some sort

of answer had to be forthcoming before
the police could, with any chance of success,
proceed upon their inquiry, and, curious to
relate, Vaughan himself seemed as it were to
have been at great pains to facilitate the
task of the authorities, for on the writing-
table in the room where the body was found,
and in the only furnished bed-room in the
house, there were scattered about settled
bills from hotels in Amsterdam, in Hamburg, in Bremen, where Vaughan had been
staying, cards of barristers whom he had
been consulting, maps of these cities, marked
in a peculiar manner with regard to the
facilities afforded for constructing new docks,
etc., etc. There was also very little doubt
about Vaughan being a well-to-do man; his
hotel bills attested that much, for all of
them bore the headings of the best establishments, while the clothes and underlinen found
in the house were of the finest. Furthermore, the dead man had all his valuables
upon him, and in less than four-and-twenty

hours after the finding of the body, when Madame Bernays had been to see it, it transpired that Henry Vaughan was really a client of her husband, although a new one; that not later than a few weeks previously he had sent him a cheque for £20 as a small refresher. The first communications between the client and the barrister had been in English, and in consequence had been overlooked or put aside as incapable of affording a clue as to the latter's whereabouts, when on the day after his disappearance his writing-table had been overhauled on the chance of finding such a clue. The theory of robbery having been thus somewhat hastily discarded, what other motive could there be for the murder of Guillaume Bernays by Henry Vaughan, who was an utter stranger to him, on the day of their first and last meeting? None. Consequently nearly all concerned were rapidly coming to the conclusion that Bernays had been the victim of an accident, as alleged by Henry Vaughan.

Nearly all. Madame Bernays was among the small minority that did not quite take things for granted. She not only doubted the probability of an accident, but intuitively suspected a connection between Henry Vaughan and Armand Peltzer. At any rate, on the evening of her return from Brussels, when the latter called to condole with her, she startled him with the abrupt remark, 'Swear to me by all you hold sacred, by the life of your child, that you do not know Henry Vaughan.' To which Armand re-replied, 'This is sheer madness; what can you be thinking of?'

Nevertheless, the police, even if they admitted the possibility of an accident, felt bound to institute an inquiry, and they began by questioning M. Almeyn, the proprietor of the house in which the tragedy occurred. The latter threw a faint light upon the subject, and so did M. Guiot, an upholsterer, who was to furnish the premises, and who, in fact, had already partly done so, but neither afforded any information likely to ensure the apprehension of Vaughan. They had no address by which to communicate with him, save that of 159 Rue de la Loi. Their combined statements repeated subsequently at the trial amounted to this. On December 2, 1881, a gentleman called upon M. Almeyn, who lives close to his property and asked to be shown over the house, with a view of taking it if suitable. He gave the name of Henry Vaughan and said he was an Australian born of an English father and a Spanish mother. He furthermore informed M. Almeyn that he was then engaged in founding a transatlantic steam service. After seeing the house, he asked for the refusal of it until December 10, in consideration of which he handed M. Almeyn the sum of 200 francs. On December 4 he again called, requesting an extension of the stipulated time for refusal, on the ground that his wife and child were very ill, and that he had not heard from them. M. Almeyn acquiesced, giving him till December 20, but on the 10th he received a letter from Hamburg finally accepting the house, and telling him that his future tenant would be with him on the 19th, when they would sign the lease. This formality was, however, not accomplished until the 21st, when Vaughan handed him six months' rent in advance, which to a certain extent obviated the taking up of his references. There appears to have been some slight difficulty about the latter, but M. Almeyn had no suspicion that there was anything wrong, attributed the misunderstanding to a mistake on the banker's part, and willingly gave Vaughan a letter of introduction to a firm of upholsterers, who were to furnish not only the house in the Rue de la Loi, but also the offices of Vaughan's company at Antwerp. While M. Guiot was preparing to execute the order, he received a letter from Vaughan, dated from London, asking him to put up the curtains throughout the front of the house, and to furnish and carpet at once two or three rooms, which he (Vaughan) indicated. Guiot had meanwhile made inquiries at Antwerp, and, finding that no one knew anything about Vaughan, he showed a certain reluctance, on the latter's return to Brussels, to go on with the business, whereupon Vaughan produced a pocket-book seemingly crammed with bank-notes. 'I suppose,' he said, 'that your bill will not exceed 50,000 francs. I will give you 15,000 in a few days. Meanwhile here's 1000 francs to go on with.

In fact, according to Guiot, Vaughan seemed in a great hurry to have at least part of the house furnished. He was, above all, anxious for a draped curtain in the passage and for another one outside the door of the back dining-room, which was to be fitted up as his business-room; so anxious as to have taken the material away with him unmade when told that the curtains could not possibly be got ready by next day. As the workmen were then in the house, he had both these curtains merely tacked up according to his own directions, and, as he said, 'temporarily.' It may be mentioned here that the medical experts afterwards stated that Bernays must have been struck while stooping to pass under the second curtain. Vaughan accounted for his hurry by saying that on January 7th — the above conversation and incidents took place on the 5th—he expected his lawyer from Antwerp, and that he wanted no workmen in the house that day. He also mentioned that several engineers from Paris and London were coming to see him, and when Guiot pointed out that it would be better to receive these gentlemen at the Hotel Britannique than in an unfurnished house, Vaughan replied that all the rooms at the hotel led into one another, and that it was very uncomfortable to talk

about important business under such circumstances.

I must apologise for a short digression
here. At the conclusion of the trial which
brought the murderers of Bernays to their
doom, the Belgian detectives greatly prided
themselves upon their skill in having unravelled the mystery. The fact is that they
unravelled nothing at all, and that but for outside aid these murderers would be still at
large. They failed altogether to fathom
the motives of Bernays's death. To use
the familiar locution, 'they saw no further
than their nose.' Starting from the idea
that Henry Vaughan was an entire stranger
to Bernays; moreover led astray by the
fact of his having spent nearly 5,000 francs
in the preliminaries of taking and partly
furnishing the house, they were almost
inclined to adopt the theory, furnished by
Vaughan himself, of accidental death.

The public, and especially the Antwerp
public, were, however, not so easily misled.

The suspicion that had struck Madame Bernays on the evening of January 19, and which found vent in the abrupt question addressed to Armand, had taken root with them also, although there is no evidence that Madame Bernays had communicated it to anyone. It was a case of spontaneous and simultaneous germination, the seed having been sown by Armand Peltzer himself during his eight years' intercourse with the Bernays family. It would be difficult to determine, after so many years, whether anyone considered Armand to be the actual murderer of Bernays, though this is scarcely likely, seeing that on the day of Bernays's death he was seen at hours ranging from Nine A.M. to late at night in Antwerp. It even transpired afterwards that he took particular care to be seen. But if public opinion had been honestly canvassed almost immediately after the finding of the body, there is no doubt that to a large extent the reply would have come in the shape of a counter-question, which in spirit, if not in substance, would have reproduced the phrase of Madame Bernays, 'Swear to me by all you hold sacred that you do not know Vaughan.' People went further still, and almost flung to Armand, upon his defence already, the words of the wolf in La Fontaine's fable, 'If it be not you, it is probably your brother.' And Armand could not, like the lamb, make answer, 'I have none.' He had several brothers, and among them one who was by no means a lamb, but a very black sheep indeed. It was Léon Peltzer, in fact, who had caused most of the sorrows of the family. It was to annul his bankruptcy that Armand had had to return from Buenos Ayres. At that time Léon was in business with another brother in Antwerp. It was Léon who afterwards left an unenviable name in commercial circles in Manchester, and defrauded Armand once more; it was he who after that compelled his brother Robert to turn him adrift at Buenos Ayres ; it was he who filled his mother's heart and mind with unspeakable grief ; it was he who, notwithstanding his great commercial abilities, found himself stranded at last in New York, and compelled to accept a situation as an inferior 'drummer'—*Anglicè*, commercial traveller—under the assumed name of Frédéric Albert. In the latter place he seemed, however, to have conducted himself more creditably.

But though known in Antwerp as a ne'er-do-well, as a swindler, as a forger, he was universally voted 'incapable of hurting a cat,' and if he had not been Armand's brother few would have suspected him of being likely to commit a mere assault—let alone a murder in cold blood. Suspecting Armand to have had a hand in the death of Bernays, people naturally began to cast about for his possible accomplice ; and considering the magnitude of the risk involved, argued, first, that Armand, if really guilty,

could not have confided such a project to
a stranger; secondly, that no stranger, of
the kind wanted for such a task, would have
lent himself to it. For this was not the
work of the mere hired assassin; the moment
the theory of an accident was discarded, the
crime assumed the proportions of the most
diabolically conceived and executed plot, the
executors of which must have been firmly
convinced of one another's loyalty to dare
even broach the first words of it.

The authorities could not long remain deaf
to these rumours, and shortly afterwards, Armand, though left at liberty, was questioned
by the magistrates as to the whereabouts of
his brother Léon. Without a moment's hesitation he stated that his brother Léon was
in America, and, in support of his statement,
produced a letter, dated St Louis, November
18, 1881, and received by him somewhere
about the time Bernays was killed. This was
meant to prove that Henry Vaughan and
Léon Peltzer could not possibly be one and

the same person, seeing that the former called upon M. Almeyn as early as December 2, etc. Nevertheless, the authorities continue their search in Europe for Léon Peltzer, and Armand is carefully watched. He knows that his correspondence is intercepted and that his every movement is recorded, and in his despair endeavours to throw the police off the scent by having his letters addressed to various friends, notably to Dr Lavisé. But the latter also has had his suspicions aroused of late, and finally informs the King's Procurator that, unknowingly, he has been the intermediary between Armand and Léon Peltzer, who, he adds, was in Brussels on that very morning (March 5). Then the game is virtually up. Armand is arrested on that day ; Léon is run to earth thirty-six hours later at Aix-la-Chapelle.

But, though arrested, three things connecting them with the death of Guillaume Bernays remain still to be proved. First, that Henry Vaughan and Léon Peltzer are one and the same person; secondly, that there was no accident, but premeditation on Henry Vaughan's part; thirdly, that Armand Peltzer was an accessory before as well as after the crime. And in successfully proving all these things the prosecution brings to light a 'masterpiece of crime,' which for ingenuity of conception and daring of execution has not its counterpart in the criminal annals of any country. The same amount of organisation, of boldness, if employed honestly, would have probably led to fame and fortune. From the moment Léon Peltzer starts for Europe, Frédéric Albert—the name by which he went in New York—is lost to everyone except to Armand Peltzer. In another month Pellat, Mario, Valgravé—all successive aliases — disappear also, and Henry Vaughan comes upon the scene; Henry Vaughan, so cleverly 'made up' for his part by the aid of a false wig, supplied by the wigmaker of the first and foremost theatre of Europe, by means of various cosmetics and a pair of blue spectacles, that Madame Peltzer would not have detected her own son under the disguise. Léon and Armand Peltzer do not believe in taking their precautions after the crime; they arrange everything beforehand. To this effect Henry Vaughan successively visits Amsterdam, Bremen, Hamburg, has interviews with celebrated barristers in all these towns, whom he pays fees and consults upon his projects, so that when Bernays has been 'killed by accident' all these barristers may come forward and become links in the chain of proof not only of the existence of Henry Vaughan, but of his social and financial position, hence of his respectability.

'Who supplied the funds for all this?' asked the prosecution. 'How came Léon Peltzer, who had not the few dollars to pay for a telegram to Europe shortly before he left—how came he in possession of thousands and thousands of francs?' And Léon answers that it is a certain Murray, the projector of the company, who supplied the funds. Unfortunately, Murray is nowhere to be found. Murray, who is the promoter of a company with a capital of a million, has no fixed address, but meets Henry Vaughan any and every where—at a café in Paris, at a public-house in London, etc. Here we find the first flaw in the comedy prepared, and the natural conclusion is that Armand has furnished the wherewithal. True, he himself was at the time in difficulties, but for such a purpose he could have found money. 'This is mere surmise,' retorts the defence. 'No,' says the prosecution; and finally proves that, though his books were in comparatively good order, 25,000 francs, which he had borrowed, had not been accounted for. Twenty-five thousand francs were, after all, not a great deal to get rid of a man whom he had learnt to hate; who, besides being the obstacle between him and the woman he loved with all his soul, had mortally insulted him; who, furthermore, kept him out of a fortune of which he stood so much in need. For Madame Bernays was a wealthy woman, and the crime committed 'in love's disguise' would have borne other fruit besides the gratification of a violent affection. No, twenty-five thousand francs were not so difficult to find, and, unfortunately for himself and his brother, Armand found them. After having proved all this, there was scarcely any necessity for the prosecution to show premeditation. If there had been, the purchase of eight different revolvers by Léon Peltzer would have been sufficient to convince the jury who found the verdict which condemned both to death.

WHEN Atreus cut up one of his nephews and served him in a fricassee to the boy's own father, the Sun, according to the Greek mythologists, turned out of his course in sheer horror at the bloody spectacle. We know well enough that this is merely a fable. The sun never went out of his way in disapproval of a human act, however gruesome, any more than he stood still at Gibeon in approval or astonishment at the quasi-religious exploit of Joshua butchering the Amorites. But the Hellenic poets wished to express their deeply-rooted execration of that particular kind of homicide which mutilates the human form divine after having taken life, and no simile borrowed from earthly existence seemed to them powerful enough for the purpose. Modern civilisation, which uses the knife, the revolver, and poison to gratify its revenge or its greed when a human being stands in its way, has still the same abhorrence, though mixed with a great deal of morbid curiosity, of that category of crime. In the course of my journalistic work I have heard, especially in England, a great deal of mawkish drivel in connection with ordinary murderers: I have never heard a word of protest against the execution of Wainwright. I cannot say what was the feeling with regard to Kate Webster, because I was not in England at the time, nor can I speak with authority about the state of public opinion in the case of Greenacre, who was executed before I was born. But I remember the murder of Harriet Lane, and a story in connection with it which confirms to a great extent what I said just now.

It happened that a few days before the trial I was talking to a detective. Now, English detectives, whatever their short-comings may be, are not bloodthirsty. When they have run their quarry to earth, they are inclined to be merciful. In this instance, however, my acquaintance was vehemently clamouring for capital punishment. He was aware that a great deal of my time was spent on the Continent, and took it for granted that I shared the lenient views of French juries with regard to crimes prompted by 'the love passion' —to use his own words. He was, above all, under the impression that the mutilation of victims was a French invention, and as such, with the insular prejudices of the middle-class Englishman, put down his foot sternly 'If the law does not make a striking example,' he said, 'we'll have that kind of thing imported here, and as it is we are already Frenchified enough. No Englishman, however cruel, however fiend-ish, would have ever hacked and butchered of his own accord, if he had not read or heard of it as a possible means of escaping detection. So up with Wainwright, I say— and I mean it.'

There was something resembling burlesque in this dislike of foreign importation, apart from the horror manifested at the heinousness of the crime itself. But my interlocutor, who was comparatively a young man, had evidently not studied his *Newgate Calendar*, else he would not have spoken so dogmatically on the subject. Mutilation of the victim after death is essentially an English invention—as far as modern times go. Of course we have heard of that Count of Toulouse who made his wife drink the blood of her troubadour lover from a cup fashioned out of his skull; tradition has bequeathed us the story of that Paris barber who cut up his victims and gave them to his neighbour, a pastrycook, who made the remains into pies, but all these authentic legends belong to the distant past. The first crime of the kind with which I am dealing at present was committed in London in the early part of the eighteenth century, and, what is more, a woman was the principal accessory to, if not the actual author of, it.

Catherine Hall was a Birmingham girl of the lower middle-classes, who, after several not very creditable adventures, succeeded in entrapping the son of her master, a farmer in Worcestershire, into a private marriage. Six years after the union young Hayes, who was evidently of as restless a disposition as his wife, came to London, where Catherine opened a lodging-house and her spouse started in the coal and chandlery trade, adding to it money-lending on portable property; for in those days pawnbroking was not subject to laws and regulations. Though fairly prosperous, Hayes's domestic life was not a pleasant one. His wife was given to fomenting quarrels among the neighbours. At times she spoke very respectfully and affectionately of her husband; at others she vilified him, and declared that she would think it no more sin to kill him than to kill a dog. After one or two peregrinations, in consequence of Mrs Hayes's proclivities to quarrel, they definitely settled in business in the Tyburn Road, now Oxford Street, whence at the end of a few years they retired to private lodgings in the same neighbourhood, Hayes having amassed a sufficient competency to make him independent of business. Meanwhile a supposed son of Catherine by a former connection, named Billings, appeared upon the scene, and led his mother into all kind of extravagance during Hayes's frequent absences from town, and about the same time the husband gave shelter to a former schoolfellow from Worcestershire, named Wood, who had left his home from fear of the press gang. Hayes himself

does not seem to have been very abstemious
or very quiet in his mode of life; there were
frequent drinking bouts at his house, and
during one of these, while in a state of
absolute stupefaction, induced by liquor, he
was supposed to have been killed by his
wife and her two accomplices. There was,
nevertheless, a struggle, for a woman named
Springate, who lodged in the room over that
where the murder was committed, heard a
violent stamping of feet, and on her going
downstairs to inquire its meaning, Mrs
Hayes replied that they had company, and
were merely enjoying themselves, but that
her friends were about to leave. It now
became imperative to dispose of the body,
and it transpired at the trial that, in the
consultation to that effect, the woman had
hit upon the idea of severing the head from
the trunk, so as to prevent the identification
of the murdered man and to baffle all
research. In the subsequent operation she
held a pail, and was most careful not to let

any blood drop upon the floor. The contents were emptied into a sink by the window, which was afterwards flushed with water. Nay, more, it was the woman who opposed the taking away of the head, and recommended the boiling of it until the flesh should part from the bones. Her recommendation was not acted upon, because her accomplices thought it would take too much time. The head was carried away by the latter, and the clanking of the pail having brought Mrs Springate to the landing once more, Mrs Hayes answered that her husband was going a journey, and, enacting her part to perfection, pretended to take leave of him, loudly regretting that he was under the necessity of going at so late an hour. Under cover of her tears and sobs, the two accomplices left the house, and eventually threw the pail into a dock near the Horseferry, Westminster. They then returned to the house to devise means for the disposal of the body. Mrs Hayes again proved the guiding spirit. It was she who suggested that it should be packed into a box and buried. A box was accordingly purchased, but, having been found too short, the body was dismembered, and crammed into it piecemeal. Fearful, however, lest its removal should attract too much attention, Mrs Hayes changed her mind at the last moment. The limbs were taken out, wrapped in a blanket, carried to a field in Marylebone, and flung into a pond.

The head had meanwhile been picked up by a lighterman belonging to the dock of the Horseferry Wharf. The authorities directed that it should be washed and the hair combed, after which it was exposed on a pole in the churchyard of St Margaret's, Westminster. A word by the way. A hundred and sixty-four years ago London was comparatively a small city, but even then the need was felt of a central mortuary, something like the Morgue in Paris, the report of which had already spread to London. That the establishment of such an institution was advocated at the time I could easily prove, just as I could prove that since then there have been several laudable efforts of the Press in that direction; still, at the time at which I write the prospect of a central mortuary is as far distant as ever. In the course of these papers I may have occasion to show what powerful aids they are in the detection of crime.

To return to my story. Among the crowds that went to see the head there were one or two who expressed their belief that it was Hayes's—a notion which, of course, was scouted by Billings and Wood, who had taken care to be among the spectators. Hayes, according to them, was out of town, and would return to London in a few days. Mr Westbrook, a chemist, was instructed by the authorities to put the head into spirits, and a few weeks elapsed, during which suspicion grew more and more rife against Mrs Hayes, notably through the agitation of a Mr Ashby, a friend of the murdered man. Being pressed by Mr Ashby, Catherine Hayes trumped up a story about her husband having killed a man in a quarrel. She alleged that the widow had consented to keep quiet on the promise of an annual allowance, which Hayes had been unable to pay, and he had therefore absconded to Portugal, whence she expected a letter from him every minute. Ashby was sceptical as to the truth of the story, and consulted a relation of Hayes, a Mr Longmore, who interviewed Catherine, and was told quite a different version of the affair. Both Ashby and Longmore took a third friend of Hayes into their confidence, and, the trio having carefully examined the head once more, there was an application to the magistrate, and Catherine Hayes, Billings, Wood, and Mrs Springate were apprehended. The latter had removed with Mrs Hayes to her new lodgings, and was suspected of being an accessory after the fact. Catherine Hayes asked to see the head, and, pretending to recognise it, asked for a lock of the hair, and on being told that she had probably had too much of his *blood* already, fell into a fit.

Curious to relate, on the very day of the arrest, the body was found by a gentleman and his servant crossing the fields at Marylebone. While the prisoners were undergoing their preliminary examination it was brought in. Billings and Wood pleaded guilty before their trial; Mrs Springate was discharged as utterly innocent of participation in the crime; Catherine had a fierce fight for her life, and after her conviction tried to poison herself, but failed; Wood died of gaol fever before the fatal day, Billings was hanged in chains, and Catherine was literally *burned alive*. The last words require some explanation. In those days, when women were burned for petty treason, it was customary to strangle them by means of a rope, which was passed round their neck and pulled by the executioner, so that they were dead before the flames could reach them.   On this occasion the executioner dropped the rope sooner than he ought to have done, in consequence of the flames reaching his hands, and Catherine Hayes's agony must have lasted at least an hour, for it took more than three hours to reduce the body to ashes.   I fancy I was right in saying that this kind of crime was an English invention, though it is but just to add that when the French took to imitating it they did so with a vengeance. What is still more odd, the other nations of the Continent scarcely took to it at all, and in England itself, we have only had three or four instances of it in the present century.

It took nearly a hundred years for the method to cross the Channel. The first Frenchman of whom we have a similar record was a lieutenant in the 4th Regiment of Light Infantry. Charles Dautun killed his aunt and his brother in the same day, though in two different quarters. The police were digging for two months, and in a circumference of not less than thirty miles, for the remains of the bodies before they succeeded in piecing them completely. He was guillotined on March 28, 1825, nearly ninety-nine years after the execution of Catherine Hayes.

More than seven years elapsed when, on August 31, 1832, a gang of lightermen unloading a cargo of tiles on the banks of the Seine, near the Hôtel de Ville, saw a man fling a box into the river and run away as fast as he could. They dived after it. It contained a head but recently severed from its trunk. Two days afterwards the latter was found in a sewer in the Rue de la Huchette, and two legs were discovered in the river near the Pont Neuf. The whole on being put together was proved to be the body of an old soldier named Ramus, employed as a collector by M. Fabre, of the Inland Revenue. Ramus had been sent on August 30 to the Treasury with about 3000 francs, and since that day had not been heard of. In a former chapter, when sketching the career of Georges Lacenaire, I reported a conversation he had with Canler, to the effect that if he, Lacenaire, had succeeded in killing Genevey and in disposing of his body, Genevey would have been suspected of having absconded with the money entrusted to him. Ramus was murdered two years before Lacenaire was apprehended, consequently Lacenaire, in counting upon the want of charity of the public in general, may have spoken from experience ; at any rate, until Ramus's head was picked up in the river—that is to say, for about sixteen hours after his disappearance—he was strongly suspected of having made off with the funds entrusted to him, and a warrant had already been applied for by M. Fabre when that gentleman received the news of his death.

As a matter of course, the police, on discovering the real state of the case, began to look for the criminal, and suspicion fell at once upon his old friend and fellow-soldier, Regey, who was then in the Paris police force, and who had been seen drinking with him on the 30th August. Regey was nowhere to be found, and they arrested his son. Having heard of the latter's fate, Regey came to Paris, and gave himself up. He confessed to having invited Ramus to his lodgings, and to having given him a dose of prussic acid in some brandy. Ramus dropped down dead, and his murderer cut him up. The difficulty was, however, to get rid of the head. Throughout we shall find that this is the stumbling-block in similar cases. At the trial Regey recanted, and ascribed the death of his old comrade to a mistake, to an accident. He was, nevertheless, beheaded on the 2nd March, 1833. In spite of his past career, of his having been decorated on the battlefield, they had to carry him to the scaffold ; he refused the administrations of the chaplain, and died the death of a coward.

Two years went by, and then within a twelvemonth from that time Europe rang with two crimes, committed under absolutely identical circumstances, allowing, of course, for the difference arising from national surroundings and characteristics. I am alluding to the crimes of Martin Lhuissier in Paris, and of James Greenacre in London.

The French upholsterer had almost as creditable a past as the English tradesman, though both were living with women not their wives. Lhuissier, unknown to Madeleine Lecomte, applied to a matrimonial agency for a legitimate spouse who might bring him a little property. James Greenacre made the acquaintance of Hannah Brown with the same intention, and, if we are to believe the evidence adduced at the trial, left his mistress, Sarah Gale, in ignorance of his projected marriage until the last moment. Lhuissier prevailed upon his intended wife to move, and to take her furniture to their new lodgings, where he killed her. James Greenacre invited Hannah Brown to come and spend Christmas Day with him, and battered her head in. Here the resemblance ceases. Greenacre takes care to dispose of the head in a place some distance from the spot where he flings part of the remains of the body. Lhuissier simply puts his victim into two separate parcels, hires a truck, and gets a commission-aire to help him load the vehicle, which both wheel as far as the Place de la Concorde, where Lhuissier gets rid of his companion on the pretext that a horse and cart is to meet him to take 'the goods' out of town to the customer for whom they are intended. For in order to give his burden the semblance of furniture he has nailed part of the body of his victim to a large sliding door of a sideboard. It matters not. Detection is sure to follow this kind of crime sooner or later, however great the precautions taken. In these two instances it followed hard upon the deed, and both men paid the penalty within a twelvemonth of one another, with this difference again, that the Englishman died game, and the Frenchman did not.

Of Joseph Huguet, who made away with his wife under similar circumstances, we need say very little. We only mention him in order to make the list thoroughly trustworthy.

When these lines first appeared in print the public were eagerly perusing the accounts of the trial of Jean Eyraud and Gabrielle Bompard for the murder of M. Gouffé, an elderly process-server in Paris; hence there is no necessity to dwell upon the particulars of that case beyond reminding the reader that, like Catherine Hayes, Eyraud packed the remains of his victim in a trunk; that, unlike Catherine Hayes, he did not change his mind at the last moment,

and dispatched them in bulk. As usual, the
glib reporter and learned leader writer—
who have, no doubt, their classics as well as
their political history at their fingers' ends,
but who, as a rule, are lamentably ignorant
of social and, above all, of criminal parallels
—were 'struck with astonishment at the
originality and daring of the scheme' when
the crime was discovered. That the French
should know nothing of the criminal annals
of England in the beginning of the eighteenth century is not very wonderful, seeing
that a writer in their best encyclopædia, in
the article 'Executions' (published 1863),
still spoke then of Tyburn and of the journey
up the Oxford Road as of actual facts; but
that the Parisian journalist should credit
Eyraud with the smallest spark of inventive
genius is inexcusable, seeing that the first
inventor of the dispatch by rail, and in a
trunk, of a murdered man was a Frenchman,
who though young and an utter novice, did
the thing so perfectly as to have left no

room for the display of ingenuity on the part of his imitators.

In 1850 there lived at the fashionable end of the Rue St Honoré a well-known dealer in art bronzes, M. Poirier - Desfontaines. Poirier - Desfontaines was an old bachelor, of very retired habits, and highly respected in the neighbourhood. He had only one servant to wait upon him, a young man, of whom little or nothing was known, and who at the same time swept the shop, put up the shutters, etc. On January 6, 1851, the place of business was opened as usual, but shortly after that the servant went out, and returned in a little while, carrying a big trunk, which he took to the private apart-ment of his master, on the first floor. Two or three hours later he told the daughter of the concierge that, his master having gone out of town for a few days, he was going to take him some clothes and a few changes of linen. At two in the afternoon he closed the shop, and with the assistance of a

M

commissionaire, brought down the trunk, which was left in the passage for a few moments while he paid the one man and engaged two others who happened to be passing with a truck. He left the house, giving everyone to understand that he was going to join M. Poirier-Desfontaines. Still, notwithstanding this official announcement, the neighbours and the concierge felt greatly surprised at M. Desfontaines's absence. He had lived in the same house for a good many years, and such a thing had never occurred before. In those days the Parisian by birth or by adoption who had strayed no further than a few miles from the capital was more common than he is now, and the old gentleman was known to be one of these. And though the concierge went to inform the commissary of police of the unusual event, the step led to nothing, because, both having examined M. Desfontaines's apartment through a pane of glass in the outer door, and having found everything apparently in 'apple-pie' order, they had fain to be content with the servant's explanation. Nevertheless, when a week elapsed and no M. Desfontaines re-appeared, a rumour of foul play became rife, and the authorities decided to have the doors forced. It became evident at the first glance that the neighbours' suspicions were well founded. The blood-stained floor of the private apartment, a cleaver equally stained with blood, left no doubt as to a murder having been committed. But the body had disappeared; and though a very active search was instituted at once, the police remained without a clue for more than a fortnight. It was only on January 30 that the Prefect of Police received a notice from the station master at Châteauroux to the following effect; A trunk had been dispatched from Paris on the 6th of that month addressed to a M. Moreaux, 22 Grande Rue. There being no person of that name at the address indicated, the sender of the goods, had been communicated with at the address given by him, at which, however, he was utterly unknown. The coincidence naturally aroused suspicion, and the Procurator of the Republic proceeded to the railway-station, where the trunk was opened in his presence. It contained the body of a man, fully dressed; the legs had been drawn up by means of a towline passed round the knees and the neck, so that the body itself and the head were lying flat against the bottom; the skull was fractured in several places. By the side of the body, which was already in an advanced state of decomposition, were found a shirt, bearing no mark, and a blood-stained pair of trousers. Both had, no doubt, belonged to the murderer, who had considered this the easiest way of getting rid of them.

When the body had been identified by the concierge of the house in the Rue St Honoré as that of M. Poirier-Desfontaines, there was virtually little to do for the police

except to apprehend the servant. There
could not be, and there was not, a moment's
doubt with regard to his guilt. In this
instance we have to record not so much a
'masterpiece of crime' as a masterpiece of
detection. Truly, the criminal had left some
traces behind, but they were slight indeed.
After much trouble, the men who had taken
away the trunk from the Rue St Honoré
were found ; but such information as they
were able to give had been practically anti-
cipated by the discovery of the body at
the station of Châteauroux. They only
furnished one other faint gleam of light.
After having booked the trunk, the servant
had booked a place for Marseilles, under the
name of Eugène Viou. This was the first
inkling the police and the public got of
the murderer's real or assumed name, for,
strange to relate, no one in the house or
in the neighbourhood had ever troubled
about it. At the booking-office of the railway in the Rue des Petits Champs some

further information was obtained. About an hour after he had booked his place Viou had returned and inquired whether the train went by way of Tours. On being answered in the negative, Viou had called a commissionaire and ordered him to shoulder his personal luggage and to take it to the Orleans Railway. After a few days' search, the porter was found, and stated that Viou had paid and dismissed him just before they came to the point Saint-Michel. He gave a description of Viou, which was superfluous, seeing that the concierge had already done so. This description was, in fact, the only thing Canler, the chief of the detective force, who had taken the case in hand himself, had to guide him.

This very clever man confessed afterwards that he was fairly puzzled. Was he to look for Viou in Tours and its neighbourhood, or was Viou's professed predilection for that cathedral town merely a trick to throw his pursuers off the scent? For a little while he was undecided which course to take, and then he had an inspiration which may be truly described as a flash of genius. In order to bring this home to the reader, I must tell him that the criminal reporter on a Paris journal is not left to shift for himself, and that the Prefecture of Police will supply him with such information as can be conveniently disclosed if he cares to apply for it. He may embellish it if he likes, but the foundation generally emanates from authentic sources. During my many years' stay in Paris as the correspondent of a London daily, I rarely failed to pay two or three visits a week to this centre of information. When something important was afoot, I often went twice in one day. Under these circumstances Canler hit upon the idea of giving the reporters a bit of fancy information. Knowing, as I have already said, that there is no more assiduous reader of the newspapers than the criminal flying for his life, Canler sent word to the

various journalists that Viou had succeeded
in crossing the Spanish frontier, and that
henceforth all further steps for his apprehension would be useless.   (Note—There
was no extradition then.)

It will be remembered that Canler had
always advocated properly directed journalism as an aid to the detection of crime,
to the tracing of the criminal.   When M.
Carlier, the then Prefect of Police, and
consequently his chief, saw the paragraph
in question, he asked himself whether he or
Canler was out of his mind, and immediately
sent for him.   'A nice muddle your valuable aids have made for us,' he began.
'You'll never lay hold of that fellow.'
Then Canler explained.   'One of two things
will occur, Monsieur le Préfet. Viou is
either in Paris or in the provinces. If in
the capital, he will remain; if in the provinces, he will return, for by this time he
has read the article, and is convinced that
his only means of safety lies in Paris.'

Canler was right. Three days later one of the inspectors came to tell the chief that Viou was staying at a *garni* in the Rue Pont-Louis-Philippe. The moment he had read the article he had returned. A few hours afterwards he was in the hands of the police. He was the last criminal executed at the Barrière St Jacques.

A careful search through the criminal annals of the Continent has convinced me that Eugène Viou was virtually the practical inventor of the 'packing and railway system' as a means of getting rid of his victim, and that his several successors merely followed in his footsteps until Barré and Lebiez, of whom I may have occasion to speak, imported an element of grim burlesque into the proceedings. But this was more than a score of years later on. Meanwhile Victor Dombey, though he does not operate until '54, is evidently inspired by Viou. When he has dispatched his victim—a Swiss wholesale dealer in watches and watch materials, whom he has decoyed to his lodgings under the pretext of giving him a large order—he quietly goes to a packing-case maker in the neighbourhood, orders a case, which is delivered the same day, 'and carefully arranges the body in it.' (The quotation marks are not mine). Then he gets a friend who is absolutely ignorant of the contents of the box to help him to carry it to the Lyons Railway, where he deposits it at the 'left luggage office.' As a matter of course, within a few days the smell in the place becomes pestilential, a commissary of police is sent for, and the crime is traced to its author. It is worthy of remark, perhaps, that both Viou and Dombey were very young men, the latter not more than twenty, and that both during their trial seemed to have looked upon the matter as a huge joke.

In Charles Avinain, who appears upon the scene twelve years later, we are confronted with a miscreant of different mettle.

He ranks with Dumollard and Lacenaire. He has the ferocity of both, and the strategical cunning and organisation of the latter. (Note—Dumollard murdered over twenty servant girls within eighteen months. Sixteen murders were proved against him at his trial).

Unlike Dumollard and Lacenaire, Avinain was a colossus. Though close upon seventy when arrested for the last time, it took seven of the most stalwart police agents, told off for the purpose, to pinion him. It was the celebrated detective, M. Claude, who ran him to earth. During the first half of 1867 scarcely a month elapsed without a quantity of human remains being found in the Seine, in, or close to, the capital. A mere glance at a map of Paris will show the reader the devious course of the river, and in those days its banks at the extremities of the metropolis were not adorned by the pretty villas and the more substantial tenements that now border them. But wherever these

remains were found they seemed to have
been dissected with a certain amount of skill,
and invariably belonged to the male sex.
Moreover, the vigorous, muscular limbs,
the sinewy arms, the somewhat coarse-
grained skin, the stalwart legs, attested that
the victims had been chosen from one class
—namely, the agricultural one. On being
carefully interrogated by M. Claude, the
medical experts furthermore admitted that,
though the severance of the limbs showed a
certain knowledge of anatomy, the process
adopted was not that of the ordinary dissecting-room. On being asked whether it might
not be that practised in the infirmaries of
convict prisons, the experts were unable to
give a positive opinion. None of them
happened to have had any experience in
that way, 'Papa Claude,' as his familiars
and admirers called him, would not be
satisfied with so vague a reply, and sent for
a prison surgeon, who gave a more definite

opinion, which to a great extent confirmed the clever detective's conjectures.

It must not, however, be imagined that the latter had arrived at these conclusions unaided or from sheer instinct. One of his subordinates had given him considerable assistance. He had discovered four different domiciles of the supposed assassin—all four situated within a stone's throw of the river, at different spots; all four bare to the verge of poverty; all four mere shanties, but adjoining large sheds in which a quantity of fodder was stored. From that moment M. Claude knew for whom to look; and an event which happened almost within four-and-twenty hours of his having reached his final conclusions still further strengthened his conviction.

Immediately after the exposure on the slabs of the Morgue of the last collection of limbs found in the Seine, a man named Duguet identified them as the remains of his father, though the head was missing.

The Paris police, however, then as now, never placed much reliance on that kind of identification, seeing there had been cases in which three or four score of people claimed the same body as that of their relative. In this instance, though, Duguet based his recognition on the peculiarly shaped and stumpy hands of the murdered man. And then a tale was unfolded which I recommend to the attentive perusal of those who are never weary of instituting comparisons between the French and the English detective forces—to the disadvantage of the latter.

On June 28 the father, according to the son, started from his farm, situated some distance from Paris (at Long-Perrier), with a heavy load of hay, intended for the weekly market at La Chapelle, then without, at present within, the city gates. At a short distance from his destination, a man, apparently ten years younger than the deceased, who was in his seventieth year, proposed to buy the load, but, not having the money upon him to settle there and then, invited him to accompany him home—taking, of course, the merchandise with him. Having spent the greater part of the day together, the purchaser purposely delayed paying until it was too late for his guest to unload and to return home, the horse having been put up meanwhile in the shed. Duguet was prevailed upon to stay for the night, during which he was struck mortally with a heavy hammer, cut to pieces, and the remains flung into the river at various places.

M. Claude, who was present while Duguet told his story to the examining magistrate, stood fairly speechless at the accuracy of the particulars. The hammer, the hatchet, the saw which he mentioned, had all been found in the tenement. For a moment it struck M. Claude that it was Duguet himself who had murdered his father, and who had dispatched all the others that had been found for the last five months. For a moment only; the solution followed hard upon the puzzle.

The graphic description of the scene, as given by Duguet, had been supplied to him by a neighbour, Farmer Lecomte, who, six months previously, had fallen into the trap set by the murderer, and had only escaped sharing the fate of so many others by his presence of mind and indomitable pluck. He had not only saved his own life, but got away with his load of hay in the morning. The police had been in possession of that information all the while, and still failed to secure the murderer. As for Lecomte himself, he was looked upon in his neighbourhood as having invented the story to account for his non-success in disposing of his produce at the market of La Chapelle. There is something in the mediæval proverb which says that a lie will travel round the world before truth can get her boots on to go in pursuit.

It must not be inferred, though, that the authorities took no steps at the time to secure the would-be murderer of

Lecomte.   They even caught sight of him
at his place in the Avenue Montaigne,
where the crime had been planned, but
before they could lay hands on him he
disappeared; it looked as if the earth had
swallowed him up.   Nevertheless, the
mere glance had been sufficient to convince one of the agents that the individual
bore a striking likeness to a ticket-of-leave
man living at Torcy under police supervision, and this slight clue was more than
enough to put M. Claude on the track.
In a short time he ascertained that the
individual in question had vanished from
the spot 'officially assigned to him as
a residence,' that his name was Charles
Avinain, that he was a butcher by trade,
and that since 1833, consequently for
a period of thirty-three years, his had
been an uninterrupted career of crime.
He also learnt that Avinain's wife and
daughter were living in one of the suburbs
of Paris, eking out a miserable subsistence

by needlework, and that since his return from Cayenne a twelvemonth previously he had paid them two visits. 'The first time,' said the daughter to M. Claude, 'he was in such a state of utter destitution as to arouse our pity. We advised him to reform, to try and get an honest living. The second time he looked so prosperous as to arouse our indignation and suspicions. Since then we have not set eyes on him.' When M. Claude returned to the Prefecture of Police, the four different domiciles of Avinain were already surrounded by the police, who felt sure, however, that he was hidden in that of the Avenue Montaigne. M. Claude repaired thither at the request of his subordinates. It is worthy of remark that during the last forty years nearly all the great chiefs of the Paris detective force have been the reverse of giants. Canler was scarcely above the middle height; Claude looked like a prosperous tradesman, incapable of any act of daring; Jacob at the first glance might have been mistaken for a hard-worked literary man or savant, wasting the midnight oil, Macé but for his beard might have passed muster as a delicate stripling; yet all these men faced the most terrible desperadoes without wincing, unarmed, provided merely with a pair of handcuffs or a walking-stick.

Claude bearded the lion in his den, accompanied by a single detective, but at the moment they were about to lay hands on him, he disappeared as if by magic, as he had done before There was a trap in the floor so cunningly devised as to defy the most practised eye at the first glance. Avinain had vanished into the sewers of the capital, hoping to escape by an outlet into the Seine. Then began a chase not unlike that described by Victor Hugo in 'Les Misérables,' at the end of which Avinain was safely got under lock and key, and rendered harmless for ever.

At the trial he did not attempt to deny his crimes, he merely objected to the accusation of having mutilated his victims; he dissected them. His face bore a sinister expression; there was a shifty look about him, but by all accounts he did not lack a certain air of distinction. He neither budged nor winced when sentenced to death, and not for a single moment did he show any signs of remorse or repentance. He bullied the executioner's assistants for their slowness and awkwardness, and his last wish was to be buried by the side of Lemaire, a parricide whose crimes were so horrible as to be unfit for publication. 'He is the only man I have ever admired,' he concluded his request.

Since then crimes of this description seem to have become more numerous throughout Europe, but the unenviable glory of leading the van in that respect still belongs to France. It is almost impossible to determine their number during the last twenty

years, because the perpetrators of at least
half of them never paid the penalty of their
misdeeds. Others, again, are so revolting
—there are degrees even in the horrible—
in their details that one dares scarcely
speak of them, such as, for instance, that of
Casimir Vignat, a farmer of Pont-Rogé
who, in 1870, cut his wife into forty pieces,
which he scattered about the dung heap, so
that the smell might not betray him. Nay.
more; to make assurance doubly sure, he asked
one of his neighbours to slaughter a diseased
sheep, and mixed the remains with those of
the woman. Two years later, when the
crime was discovered, the authorities were
compelled to turn up more than ten acres of
land which he had manured 'with his com-
posite preparation,' to use Vignat's expression. It took ever so many months to
reconstitute the human skeleton. Of Isaac
Sitbon, who, I believe, was arrested in
London in 1872, and his accomplice Tole-
dano, we need say little. They murdered

and dismembered a Marseilles merchant
for sheer greed, and Vaux, of Geneva,
whose crime dates from the same year, calls
for no special comment. There is merely a
repetition of the same process, and, but for
the horror these acts inspire, one might say
of their inventors and the latter's imitators
what Voltaire said of the versifiers who
compare a pretty woman's mouth to a rose-
bud 'The first who made use of the simile
was a poet, the others are imbeciles.'

Billoir's crime comes undoubtedly under
the heading of 'Imitations,' and as such
would not deserve a lengthy description but
for the element of burlesque which was in-
voluntarily introduced into it, and which
convulsed Paris with laughter for days.
The element, in fact, was so strong as to
have condoned the laughter. To myself it
is as welcome as a bit of farcical comedy in
a gloomy transpontine melodrama. I have
mentioned before now the wonderful instances of pseudo-identification resulting from

the exposure of an incomplete or even complete body at the Morgue. There had been sons who after their demise found twice as many fathers as Captain Marryat's hero Japhet during his life ; there had been sires who found as many offspring as the Biblical patriarchs, most blessed in that respect, and many more than that prolific Bulstrode of Cromwell's and Charles II's time who had two score and ten. The sisters, the cousins, and the aunts, not to mention the friends, male and female, of Billoir's victim would have frightened even a Captain Corcoran of H.M.S. *Pinafore*. They amounted exactly to the number of olive-branches, legitimate and illegitimate, of that King of Poland surnamed 'the Strong'—*i.e.*, one hundred and eighty-three.

On November 8, 1876, a party of children disporting themselves on the rafts of the Seine near St Ouen, which are placed there for the purpose of collecting the vegetable and other refuse floating down the river, noticed a large bundle wrapped in some dark material. The tide was low, but, unable to get it out unaided, an urchin appealed to a couple of working men who happened to be passing. The bundle contained the head and trunk of a woman. The latter had been severed below the waist and disembowelled; the former was completely shaved. A search was immediately set afoot, and the lower part of the body, with the legs, dragged up a few hours afterwards. The body had been hacked in twain simply. Transported to the Morgue, the farce of indentification began. According to one visitor the body was that of an Arab woman belonging to a band of mountebanks. Four-and-twenty hours later the Arab woman was discovered to be pursuing her avocations at a fair about thirty miles away from Paris. Next morning half-a-dozen inhabitants of the Rue Rochechouart waited upon the chief detective, and insisted that the body was that of the wife of a shoemaker, who, having had a quarrel with her husband, had mysteriously disappeared. In a short time the shoemaker's wife was discovered to be living in another quarter of Paris, and on the eve of presenting her husband with another olive-branch. Pending the inquiries necessary to verify these various statements, a gentleman from Tours telegraphed that his maidservant had gone out one evening a fortnight previously, that she had not returned since, and asked for a photograph of the murdered woman to be sent to him. The request was complied with; the gentleman recognised the likeness, there was no doubt in his mind; it was that of the missing domestic.

The news spread like wildfire through the capital of Touraine, when, lo! and behold, the young woman made her appearance at the house of her former master—to fetch away her box! A cook residing at Ville d'Avray swears that the photograph is the likeness of her dearest bosom friend. M. Jacob rushes away to the suburbs, brings

back the cook to the Morgue, and, notwithstanding the late hour, has the gas lighted.
The woman bursts into tears and wildly sobs,
' Yes, it is my own dear friend Clémence ; I
recognise her gown. I have always told
her that her love escapades would prove her
ruin.' Requested to explain more fully, she
states that the murdered woman's name is
Clémence Barbari, that she was the mistress
of a private quartered at the Camp of Ville-
neuve-l'Etang. She supplies full particulars
of the soldier ; M. Jacob rushes to the
barracks ; the soldier confirms the statement
of the cook, but, to make assurance doubly
sure, asks to be taken to another barracks,
at Rueil this time, to submit the photograph to a comrade who succeeded him in
the affections of Clémence Barbari. According to this third witness, the likeness of
the murdered woman to Clémence Barbari
admits of no doubt, and he gives the address
of Clémence. Another rush on M. Jacob's
part. When he reaches the Rue Lamartine

he is informed that Clémence has moved within the last few days to the Boulevard de Strasbourg. M. Jacob is off once more, urging his driver to make haste. He scampers up four flights of stairs, and, breathless with fatigue and excitement, rings the bell. The door is opened to him —by Clémence Barbari in the flesh.

Nevertheless, it was the photograph that led eventually to the identification of the victim and to the arrest of the criminal. There are periodical waves of emotion that sweep over the French capital like the periodical fits of respectability which, according to Macaulay, stir British society to its very depths. The obvious cause is by no means commensurate with the effect produced, and this is what happened in the present instance. Vignat had cut his wife in forty odd pieces, and treated the remains with a revolting cynicism, scarcely exceeded by the cannibalism of the prehistoric Atreus and the mediæval Comte de Toulouse, and only equalled by that god-fearing Benjamite who divided the Levite's wife into twelve lumps and sent them like so many slices of wedding cake, or cartes-de-visite to the different tribes; and yet Vignat's crime had aroused no feeling of horror like that of Billoir, who only 'halved' his victim. It is a problem for the psychologists to solve. I only state the fact, and not from hearsay, for at the time I happened to be in Paris for a few days. The photographs of the murdered woman were sold in thousands, and one facetious journalist wrote an article purporting to be the complaint of various shopkeepers, charging the police with unfair competition in the sale of Christmas novelties and New Year's gifts. Among the purchasers was the *habitué* of a *café* on the Boulevard Orano. Proud of his acquisition, he showed it in the evening to his fellow *habitués*. 'I say,' exclaimed someone all of a sudden, 'this is the wife of the *décoré. Décoré* means a man who wears an order, and the individual thus designated was an old soldier, who wore the ribbon of the 'military medal' in his button-hole. The military medal, I should add, is not lavished broadcast. The police were immediately communicated with, but no one seemed to know the name of the *décoré*. Nevertheless, he was unearthed in a few hours. Sebastian Billoir had distinguished himself on the battlefield, and he strenuously denied having committed the deed. He recognised the portrait as that of his former mistress, Marie le Manach. The authorities, mindful of his honourable past, and of his reiterated protestations that he did not know what had become of his former mistress, were on the point of setting him at liberty, in spite of the incessant clamour of the Press, which refused to believe in his innocence, and insisted upon the cesspool in Billoir's house being emptied. The police yielded at last, and twenty-three days after

the arrest of Billoir the intestines and hair
of Marie le Manach were found there.
When Billoir was informed of this he sent
in hot haste for M. Jacob, and confessed
that Marie le Manach had come home
drunk in the night of November 6-7. She
had broken a glass by which he set great
store, he had given her a kick in the abdo-
men, and she had fallen down dead. Then,
and only then, according to him, he had cut
her in two and flung her body into the river.
But the medical expert for the prosecution
opposed a formal denial to this; he strenuously maintained that Marie le Manach
was literally hacked to death, in proof
whereof he showed that the body did not
contain an ounce of blood, which could not
have been the case if she had been mutilated
when life was extinct, because immediately
after life is extinct the blood sets and ceases
to flow. The professor went so far as to
say in open court, 'I swear that this man
is guilty'; and Billoir on hearing his death

sentence, exclaimed, 'it is medical science which has murdered me.'

Though more than thirteen years have elapsed since Billoir's execution it is a moot point still whether Marie le Manach did not fall into a dead swoon, and whether Billoir under the impression that she was really dead, did not cut her up from fear of detection. It would have scarcely lessened his guilt; unfortunately there was no trace of the alleged kick. Billoir died like an old soldier, staunch to the last.

Our list of predecessors of Wainwright ought to have stopped before Billoir, but he fitly closes it. He, more that any of the others, perhaps, is deserving of some compassion, because, whether we accept his own version or that of the prosecution, his crime was undoubtedly committed in a moment of passion, and was not inspired by motives of greed that prompted nearly all, from Catherine Hayes's to Vignat's. He had nothing to gain by Marie le Manach's death.

Of those that come after him two only could be dealt with in these papers,* if space permitted, for we cannot speak of Maestdag, of Antwerp, who cut his wife into a hundred and thirty-three pieces, and literally boiled the flesh off the bones—as Pel did five years ago, as Lacenaire would have done had he succeeded in killing Genevey, the banker's porter. There is a limit even in the narration of the horrible, and the crimes of Menesclou, Vitalis and Marie Boyer, and Mielle are beyond that limit. The particulars of their misdeeds can scarcely be mentioned with bated breath.

---

* These papers originally appeared in *The Weekly Dispatch*, the Editor of which has kindly permitted their reproduction in book-form.

AN ANONYMOUS MASTERPIECE

Aʙᴏᴜᴛ the middle of 1839 an ironmaster hailing from the department of the Corrèze —or, to speak more correctly, from the province of Lower Limousin—came to Paris in search of a wife. The unsophisticated English reader might infer from this that M. Pouch-Lafarge was either too fastidious to choose from among the eligible spinsters of his own province, or that he was better known in the drawing-rooms of the capital than in those of his immediate neighbourhood. This was by no means the case. So great a stranger was he to Parisian circles as to have to apply for assistance in quest of the desired helpmeet to a then famous matrimonial agency. Nor did he appear to have been particular with regard to the personal charms of his future spouse, for the principal of the De Foy Institution subsequently stated that his patron would have allowed him a vast latitude in the matter of age and appearance—that his main concern evidently was a considerable marriage portion. In fact, it was the anxiety for substantial advantages to be derived from his projected union that had driven M. Lafarge so far afield in search of a bride. They were probably not to be obtained in the vicinity of Tulle, where he carried on operations, and where his financial embarrassments were well known. In one word, M. Lafarge wanted money to meet his pressing engagements, also to pursue his experiments with regard to a new process of melting, for which he was anxious to obtain a patent. He would have been willing to take the patent without the wife; he was not prepared to take the wife unless she had the means of getting him the patent.

It was never accurately known whether M. Lafarge met the unfortunate lady who became his wife in the drawing-rooms of the matrimonial agent, or whether that individual had had any hand in the arrangements of the marriage; one thing only is certain, that five days after his first introduction to Mdlle. Marie Cappelle the banns were published. Marie Cappelle, the reverse of her intended husband, was a familiar figure in very good Paris society; she was exceedingly well connected, not strictly good-looking, but withal fair to look upon, highly educated, and what was better than all in the eyes of M. Lafarge, possessed of 100,000 francs. Her paternal aunt, with whom she lived—her father and mother being both dead—had married M. Garat, the secretary of the Bank of France. In short, she must have been considered at the time, as she would be considered at present, a very good match ; and still she married a man in no way distinguished socially or mentally, in spite of his pseudo-inventive qualities—a man, moreover, on the verge of bankruptcy. It was afterwards alleged that these monetary difficulties were not known to the family of Mdlle. Cappelle—that M. Lafarge had, as it were, enacted the Claude Melnotte with his affianced wife, had spoken of Le Glandier as a magnificent estate, and of his home as of a veritable palace ; but to anyone more or less intimately acquainted with the habits and customs obtaining at French marriages then as well as now, this is scarcely credible. It wanted the gullibility of theatrical audiences to swallow the first Lord Lytton's play of the ' Lady of Lyons,' though, after all, it is doubtful whether French audiences would have thus swallowed it. It is altogether contrary to the reality

A frankly impecunious nobleman may win the heart of the daughter of a retired tradesman in France, and induce

the parents to open their purse-strings
for the sake of the ' brilliant alliance',
but the parents will do so with their
eyes open. Should the aspirant bridegroom
pretend to have means, their source will be
strictly investigated. Marie Cappelle, however, was not the daughter of a retired
tradesman, nor was Lafarge the bearer of an
historic name. There was nothing to dazzle
her or her friends. She was sentimental
and romantic, as we shall show immediately,
but was Lafarge the ideal of such a girl's
dreams? That a man like M. Garat, the
secretary of the Bank of France, with every
facility for inquiry, should not have investigated the position of the future husband of
his niece and ward must and will always remain a strange instance of neglect, unless
we accept the theory, broached afterwards,
that Mdlle. Cappelle was not absolutely spotless, and that her friends were
anxious to get her married. The proof of
this assertion was certainly not conclusive

at the subsequent trial; but, as this is a part
of the mystery which has never been solved
no positive opinion is possible, though I
may have to refer to it again. For the
present we will accompany the newly-wedded
couple to their home in a distant province,
for which they started on their very wedding-day. It would appear that almost at
the first stage of their journey young
Madame Lafarge became aware of the incompatibility of tone and manners between
herself and her husband. The young girl,
whatever might have been her moral worth,
had been brought up amidst refined surroundings; the husband had the uncouth bearing,
the brutal familiarity, of the provincial, which
even in our days of railway travelling and
rapid communication marks the difference between the Parisians and the rural populations,
from the highest to the lowest classes. At
Orleans, where they stayed for the night,
Monsieur Lafarge entered his wife's room,
though he was told by her maid that

Madame was in her bath. His reply showed a want of delicacy to which Mdlle. Cappelle had been a stranger in her own home. And when they reached the magnificent country estate and the palatial mansion situated thereon, the former was found to be a wilderness, the latter scarcely more than a poorly furnished brick tenement, devoid of every comfort, and unfit for the habitation of a delicately-reared girl. Young Madame Lafarge was absolutely horror-stricken at the deception practised upon her, and even attempted her own life. She refused to communicate personally with her nominal husband—for he was no more than that at the time—begging him to let her go, to keep her dowry, but to restore her to her friends. She gave him plainly to understand that she would strongly oppose any attempt on his part at cohabitation. This latter announcement, however, appears to have had an effect the very opposite to that wished for—a reconciliation took place, which may have been perfectly honest on both sides, but which was afterwards stigmatised as a profound piece of dissimulation on Marie Lafarge's side. There was not the slightest evidence to support this view of the case, but as we proceed we shall become aware that throughout the whole of this tragedy there was a display of relentless rancour on the part of Madame Lafarge's accusers which would have never been tolerated by public opinion anywhere but in a French provincial town, where political passion was, and is still, imported into every debate, into every incident of daily existence.

We have said that there was not the slightest evidence of Marie Lafarge's alleged dissimulation; we may go further still, and positively maintain that there was every proof of her perfect sincerity. Her letters to her female friends in Paris, at first very sad, become gradually more cheerful, and at last teem with clever sketches of provincial life.   Her husband, at first very repugnant to her, is making headway in her affections. Beneath the coarse husk she begins to see the sterling qualities, the indomitable energy, of the man ; in short, if not intensely happy, she is evidently determined to make the best of a bad bargain, and to abandon all idea of crying over spilt milk.   It is at this very period that the husband and wife make their respective wills, endowing one another with their worldly goods, and, though no proof is forthcoming that the step has been suggested by the young wife, or what possible benefit she could derive from it, it is subsequently used as a weapon against her.   Her prosecutors—persecutors would be the more correct term—wither her with their contempt, but the woman who clandestinely opened her daughter - in - law's testamentary document, who broke the seals and divulged its contents, is held up to admiration.

Four or five months after the marriage the husband goes to Paris, provided with the wife's signature to contract a loan on her property, and to take out the patent for the invention that has haunted his sleep for the last few years. Though unknown in French society, M. Lafarge is a familiar figure with almost every money-lender and bill dis-counter in Paris, for, aided by his factotum, Denis Barbier, he has scarcely done any-thing else but 'fly kites' for the last eighteen months previous to his union; kites drawn or accepted—often both—by men of straw, in the finding of whom Barbier has no rival. Though Barbier does not ac-company his employer this time, he dis-appears twenty-four hours after the latter's departure from Le Glandier, and is seen in his company in the capital. Later on it transpired that 30,000 francs'-worth of ac-commodation bills had been discounted, the proceeds of which are absolutely missing, and no trace of which is ever found.

For the present, we must confine our attention to M. Lafarge, who, on December

18, receives a letter from his mother, apprising him of the dispatch of a box of cakes which he is asked to eat at a certain hour, 'in affectionate remembrance of the dear ones at home.' When the box arrives, it is found to contain, not a number of small cakes but one very large one. M. Lafarge, thinking, no doubt, that women's proverbial fickleness of mind might apply to cakes as well as to other sweet things of which she is supposed to be the dispenser, unsuspectingly ate a small piece of the one sent, and was immediately seized with violent colic. He appears to have rallied somewhat during the next fortnight, but there is no doubt about his having been in a dying state when he reached Le Glandier on January 5, where he died nine days later. Denis Barbier had returned a few days before M. Lafarge.

It was never ascertained who cast the first suspicion on the unhappy Marie Lafarge, but it was certainly not the medical man who had attended the husband for years.

He ascribed Lafarge's death to nervous colic, to which his patient had always been subject. A second doctor who was called in shortly before Lafarge's death gave it as his opinion that an egg-posset, prepared by the wife, showed traces of arsenic. He never made it clear, though, why, this being the case, he allowed his patient to take it, and why he did not draw the attention of the other members of the family to the fact. Some of the latter, including Lafarge's mother, encouraged, however, by the statement of this wonderful son of Æsculapius, testified to their having seen the wife mix on several occasions a white powder with the invalid's food, and to her having sent at three different times for a considerable quantity of arsenic to a chemist in the neighbourhood. Denis Barbier confirmed the latter statement, adding that he had been the messenger each time, and that Madame Lafarge had given him a letter to the chemist, recommending him to keep the matter a secret. The poison, she said, was wanted to kill the rats that infested Le Glandier. Interrogated on the subject, Madame Lafarge did not deny having sent for the arsenic, but maintained that it had been handed to a maid-servant with instructions to mix it with some food into balls, and to scatter it about the place for the vermin to devour. Several of these balls were analysed, but contained no arsenic whatsoever. Then the servant came forward and confessed to having buried the packets of arsenic in the garden, instead of employing their contents as she had been directed to do. The packets were accordingly dug up, but only contained powdered bicarbonate of soda. Thereupon a post-mortem examination was demanded by the family of the deceased man. The first experiments were inefficiently conducted. The medical men of Tulle entrusted with the analysis reported the existence of a great quantity of arsenic in the intestines. Examined as to the process by which these results had been obtained, they admitted having boiled the digestive tube and some of the viscera, which had yielded a yellowish down-like precipitate. The latter proving to be soluble in ammoniac, they had concluded it to be of an arsenical nature. Orfila, the eminent chemist, pronounced the analysis to have been insufficient. According to him, the precipitate obtained, which after all, might be only an animal substance very frequently met with in bile, ought to have been still further reduced to metallic arsenic. Hence, everything had to be done over again. Meanwhile, the greater part of the viscera that might have contained the suspected arsenic had been absolutely wasted.

It is scarcely necessary to insist upon the excitement caused by the publication of these and other details before the trial. We have had an instance of that kind of thing in our minds not very long ago, but

it would be a deliberate insult to the Liver-
pool of the present day to compare it to the
Tulle of 1840.   Both towns were swayed
by unreasoning passion, and in both instances reckless statements, for and against,
were bandied about, but while in the
English cultured centre passion and statements sprang throughout from a sincere
conviction as to the accused woman's guilt
or innocence, from an honest determination
to get at the truth, the whole truth, and
nothing but the truth, the strife in the
hole-and-corner French borough was en-
gendered and fanned into a blaze by a sentiment which is the meanest on earth when
it exceeds the limits assigned to it by modern
sociology—political resentment.   And that
this was the case at Tulle there is not the
slightest shadow of a doubt.   After the
lapse of half a century it becomes difficult
to determine why the authorities, by which
I do not only mean the judicial authorities
but all the representatives of that ' officialism '

which is still the curse of France, especially
in the provinces, were bent upon convicting
and condemning Marie Lafarge. That they
were thus bent is proved by their having
replaced at the last moment the counsel for
the prosecution (the Advocate-General) by
a colleague from a distant jurisdiction, because he, the former, was suspected of
sympathy with the prisoner. It was surmised at the time that the child was suffering for the sins of the parent; General
Baron De Cappelle, Marie Lafarge's father,
had been not only a general of Napoleon,
but, after the latter's fall, an inveterate and
active opponent of the succeeding dynasties.
I do not vouch for the accuracy of this
statement, but one thing is certain. Public
opinion, which was almost unanimously in
favour of Marie Lafarge, was not altogether
prompted by a feeling of compassion for a
possibly innocent woman; its only love
sprang largely from its only hate—in other
words, from the opposition, always more or

less rancorous in France, of the powers that
be. From my personal experience in later
cases, I am convinced that if the authorities
had seen fit to adopt an attitude different
from what they did, the sympathy on the
part of the public would have been, if not
less strong, perhaps, at any rate less blatant.
And I am equally convinced that had there
been less clamour on the one side there
would have been less persecution on the
other.

That this spirit of persecution pervaded
the whole of the trial, which began on
September 2, 1840, it would be difficult to
deny. Fifty years have gone by, and the
'Lafarge case' is still quoted as a disgrace
to the French Bench, which, not content
with seeing a woman of gentle birth, amiable
and accomplished, stand in the dock branded
as a poisoner, must needs charge her with
crimes, less heinous perhaps, but decidedly
more degrading. For, even if her guilt in
the one respect had been as clear as daylight,

circumstances morally extenuating might have been found in the conditions of her marriage when we consider that in those days there was no divorce law in France, and that a young woman of her position, inveigled into a union such as hers had been might have been goaded by despair into an attempt on the deceiver's life in the hope of snapping the bond she could not legally undo. But to charge such a woman with petty larceny, with breach of trust, with embezzling the diamonds of one of her friends, was the most heartrending exhibition of rancorous spite, the most disgusting display of predetermined contempt of justice recorded in modern civilisation. And yet these were virtually the charges set forth in the preamble to the indictment. Not only had Marie Cappelle previous to her marriage pilfered articles of value from her aunt and uncle's drawing-room, but she had also made away with the diamonds entrusted to her by Mdlle. de Nicolai. The latter, it ap-

peared, had had an ante-nuptial *liaison* with
a young Spaniard named Félix Clavé.
Shortly after she became the Viscountess
De Léotaud she went to the theatre one
night, and there saw her former admirer
among the banner - bearers and super-
numeraries—at any rate, in a very humble
position. Dreading Clavé's revelations, or
perhaps in order to recover her letters to
him, she had charged Marie Cappelle to
open negotiations, and, being short of money
had handed her some family diamonds, with
the proceeds of which she was to effect the
wished for surrender of the love epistles.
The diamonds were certainly proved to have
been in the possession of Madame Lefarge
at some period after her marriage, but when
the police, who had been entrusted with the
tracing of the thief by M. de Léotaud,
asked her point-blank what had become of
them, she refused to give an answer. She
defied M. de Léotaud to substantiate the
charges. There was no attempt to do so,

and after a few months of coolness between
the two women, their old friendship was
resumed. It was only during the preliminary investigations instituted by the prosecution that Madame Lafarge gave the above
account of the affair, and sent Maître
Lachaud, one of her counsel, to Madame
de Léotaud to beg of her to tell the
truth. It was about the worst thing she
could have done, for the lady's admission of
Madame Lafarge's version would have in-
culpated her in her husband's eyes, and as
a matter of course she strenuously denied
everything. According to her, the whole
tale was a fabrication. She had certainly
known a M. Clavé, and corresponded with
him, but there had been no need on her
part to buy his silence, for, first of all, the
letters were of the most innocent description, and secondly she had not seen M.
Clavé since 1836. Nevertheless, the trial
had scarcely begun when there arrived a
letter from a M. Clavé, a government

official in Algeria. He had seen the accounts in the papers, and he distinctly stated as follows: In 1839 there had been delivered to him by mistake a small case, of the contents of which he remained ignorant, but which he had after some inquiry handed over to a namesake, M. Félix Clavé also resident in Algeria. The latter, in thanking him, said that it was a box he had been expecting for some time from a lady friend, Viscountess de Léotaud. This revelation ought to have made the prosecution pause; not only did they not cite either the first or second M. Clavé, but they refused to adjourn the trial so as to enable the defence to do so.

Nor was this all. Accusations of pre-nuptial immorality were scattered broadcast against Marie Lafarge. One young fellow with whom she was thus said to have committed herself, on hearing the grave position of the lady, blew his brains out. The letters found at his domicile were tender and affectionate, but they proved nothing more than a romantic, though essentially platonic, attachment.

Meanwhile the evident wish to hurry on the proceedings that had prompted the refusal to wait for the evidence of the Clavés was made manifest in more points than one; in fact, until the very end. The principal point upon which the prosecution relied was the presence of arsenic in the body of Lafarge. The first analysis having been proved to be valueless, a second was ordered. This time it was made according to the instructions of Orfila, at the very moment when the counsel for the prosecution was addressing the jury. (Note—In French criminal procedure, the prosecution addresses the jury after the indictment has been read and the witnesses, as well as the accused, have been interrogated by the President of the Court). Not a trace of arsenic was found. The counsel for the prosecution said that the contradiction between the two reports was too flagrant to be admitted, and demanded a third analysis. It was the celebrated Dupuytren who undertook the third experiment, with results similar to those of the second. Still the Court was not satisfied, and sent for Orfila from Paris to make a final analysis. The latter concluded that there was a certain quantity of arsenic, but so insignificant as to be termed imponderable. Thereupon Raspail was fetched from Paris in hot haste by the defence, but too late—the verdict had already been given. And notwithstanding his emphatic declaration that he would undertake to extract from the legs of the President's chair a quantity of arsenic equal to that extracted by Orfila from the body, the motion of appeal was rejected. Madame Lafarge was not condemned to death ; the judges stopped at judicial or pseudo-judicial murder. She was sentenced to penal servitude for life, and to be publicly exposed in the market-place at Tulle. The witnesses against her were morally as well as physically upheld by the Court. Not a whisper was allowed against them. The embarrassed financial situation of Lafarge was slurred over. Denis Barbier was held up as a model of rectitude and honesty, though there is little doubt that he was the murderer. The defence wished to examine him with regard to the 30,000 francs, the proceeds of the accommodation bills discounted in Paris, which had disappeared together with 25,000 francs borrowed by Lafarge on his last homeward journey from the solicitor of Madame Lafarge on the latter's signature. The defence was brow-beaten and silenced. In vain did it point out that the case containing the cake had been tampered with on its journey to Paris, or at any rate before it reached Lafarge, seeing that it was opened before he entered the room; in vain did it point out that the arsenic had been in Barbier's possession before it reached his mistress, and that he might have substituted the bicarbonate of soda, seeing that he and not Madame Lafarge was the accomplice of the ironmaster in his shady bill transactions which amounted to forgeries; in vain did it do all this. The motion for appeal was rejected, and Madame Lafarge was incarcerated at Montpellier, where she languished for twelve years, during which almost every person of note visited her. Rachel, the celebrated actress, spent a whole day there, reciting the most magnificent pieces of her repertory for the amusement of the unhappy woman. Anicet Bourgeois and Dennery proclaimed her innocence from the stage in ' La Dame de St Tropez,' which some of my readers may remember to have seen in its English garb during the late Alfred Wigan's lesseeship of—I believe—the Olympic. M. Dennery still points with pride to a sofa cushion in his drawing-room, which was embroidered by Marie Lafarge in her prison and sent to him in recognition of his noble efforts in her behalf. Maitre Bac, one of her counsel, openly offered to marry her if the Government would grant her a free pardon. It was all of no avail. For eight years during Louis Philippe's reign, for four more during the Second Republic, a woman expiated the crime, not of having poisoned her husband, but of being the daughter of a staunch adherent of the Napoleonic dynasty. She, as well as her husband—and perhaps less deservedly than he—was the victim of an anonymous 'masterpiece of crime' than which there has been no more daring, no more carefully-planned, no more dramatic in modern days.

It is to the credit of the Third Napoleon that one of his first acts of power was the liberation of Marie Lafarge. But, alas, it was too late! She was transported in a dying state to Ussat, where she expired a few months later. Her own family shortly after her conviction applied for a warrant against Denis Barbier, who, at that time was always prowling around the prison. The authorities refused to grant it. As for

Félix Clavé, the only one who could have shed some light on the affair of the diamonds, he died in the Pau lunatic asylum a twelvemonth after Marie Lafarge.

A MASTERLY DÉBUT

Early in the morning of the 20th September 1869, M. Langlois, a farmer at Pantin, one of the eastern suburbs of Paris, was strolling through his fields when he noticed a small mound or hillock, which, he felt sure, had not been there the day before. On looking more closely at it, he finds, that though the soil has been undoubtedly disturbed, there has also been an attempt to make it re-assume its former condition by systematic trampling and the tracing of cleverly simulated furrows across it. Impelled by curiosity rather than by a serious suspicion of evil, M. Langlois mechanically takes up a spade and begins to dig when in a few minutes he lays bare the body of a woman, frightfully mutilated and in a few moments more those of five children, the eldest of which was not more than sixteen, while the youngest, a girl, seemed to have been between three and four. The mother, to all appearance very powerfully built, had been wounded in forty-eight different places, the face had been stabbed and hacked out of all recognition while the head was almost severed from the trunk by one blow of a hatchet. The face of the eldest child, a boy, was not so horrible to look upon ; he had evidently been strangled, and looked as if death had come to him while asleep, albeit that the hair which stood positively on end, the half-closed and swollen eyelids, the distended nostrils showed that the moment between life and death had been one of agonising terror. His three brothers and sister had apparently been spared that ordeal, the murderer having been too quick ; before they could realise the situation, they were lifeless, or at any rate unconscious, their faces like that of their mother being simply so much lacerated flesh. The subsequent evidence of the medical experts, however, added a greater horror to the whole by proving conclusively that at least five out of the six victims had been huddled beneath the sod before life was extinct.

As may be imagined, farmer Langlois did not stop to observe a tithe of all this ; his first thought was to inform the nearest authorities ; the news spread rapidly and in less than two hours the whole of the capital seemed to be wending its way to the hitherto quiet outskirt. Without wishing to depreciate the acknowledged ability of the Paris detective force during the latter part of the Second Empire, and least of all that of its celebrated Chief, M. Claude, the impartial chronicler is bound to state that the initial steps towards the discovery of the author of the crime were by no means attended with difficulty. The identity of the victims admitted of no doubt from the very beginning; the first and foremost clue being the name of the provincial tailor on the buttons of the boys' clothing There was no need, though, to apply to the Roubaix clothier for information. Even in the *blasé* Paris of '69 a sextuple murder was a sufficiently extraordinary event to set all tongues wagging, and before long the police were apprised that late in the afternoon of the 19th September a woman answering the description of the murdered one, accompanied by five children, had engaged two rooms for the night at the Hotel du Nord opposite the Northern Railway Station. She had asked for a person of the name of Jean Kinck, and a young fellow of that name was staying there at the time and had been for the last few days. Finding that he was absent for the moment, the woman had merely left her luggage, consisting of a large basket, saying that she would return in a few hours. She had been noticed afterwards in the neighbourhood, strolling along with her five children and gazing at the shop windows, but neither she nor any of the little ones bought anything. Upon her body was found a photograph which the manager and the attendants at the Hotel du Nord at once declared to be the portrait of the young man who was entered in their books as 'Jean Kinck, Engine Fitter, coming from Roubaix.' Further inquiries brought to light the fact of the same young fellow having purchased in the afternoon of the 19th at an ironmonger's in the neighbourhood a pick and a spade.

The distance from the Northern Railway to the erstwhile barrier of Pantin is roughly speaking between five and six miles, the field in which the crimes were committed was about a third of a mile further on. How were the family of six besides the murderer himself, conveyed to the spot and by whom? The police perceived plainly enough that this was the first thing to be ascertained and set to work accordingly.

Pantin never was nor is it ever likely to be a fashionable quarter, albeit that during the seventeenth and eighteenth centuries it was dotted with a goodly number of country seats. In such a place a cab is sure to attract attention at no matter what hour of the day When it happens to make its appearance at an advanced hour of the night it becomes little short of a phenomenon, provided there be any inhabitants awake to see it pass. In default of these it is sure to arouse the vigilance of the policeman on duty, even if it escape the notice of the excise officer who is always on guard at the gates of the French capital and who is not only a lynx-eyed individual but afflicted with a Uriah Heepish thirst for knowledge where the tricks of the inventive smuggler are concerned. He, the excise officer, has before now flashed his bull's eye on a cabful of seemingly jolly good fellows professing quite in a casual way to be going to a suburban restaurant or tavern a few hundred yards down the road to keep up the birthday or the wedding anniversary of a friend; he has seen the empty carriage return half-an-hour or twenty minutes later and allowed it to go unquestioned on its way—to his cost, or rather to that of the fiscal authorities; the returning vehicle being simply a clever reproduction of the other, but so fitted as to contain ever so many gallons of spirits.

The police, therefore, were not far wrong in appealing in the first instance to the excise officers for information; they took it for granted that the murderer could not have conveyed his victims by any other means than that of a cab. The ironmonger who had sold the pick and the spade, stated that though the implements had been purchased as early as five in the afternoon, they had not been taken away before eight in the evening. The nature of the wounds inflicted on the victims made it more than probable that they must have bled profusely, yet in turning over the soil, it was found to be scarcely discoloured and during the night of the 19-20th September the weather had been such as to prevent the blood, if there had been any, from being absorbed, hence, the theory of the police, which proved to be correct, that the enormous ditch that held the victims had been dug before, not after they were dispatched. On being measured the excavation proved to be at least ten feet long, nearly two feet deep and three feet wide. The murderer was not likely to have set about these preliminaries with his victims waiting a couple of hundred yards away ; he had proceeded to Pantin alone, done his work and returned to fetch the mother and her five children. By that time it must have been late and the omnibusses to these outlying parts have ceased plying. It was almost certain then, that the murdered family had been taken to Pantin in a cab.

Acting upon the not illogical deduction, the police, as has been said already, applied to the excise office at the Pantin Gate for information—but without results. The murderer was evidently as clever as the police and had abstained from courting awkward notice either by stopping the vehicle at, or having it driven through, the city gates. He had taken his victims through on foot, and solitary as was the place, this might easily be accomplished without arousing undue suspicion. Incoming pedestrians are subject to search, not outgoing. Even the former, carrying no parcels are allowed to proceed unhindered.

Chance, however, befriended the police. One of their own agents had noticed a heavily laden cab rattling along the high road. The constable averred that he had endeavoured to stop the vehicle, inasmuch as it carried nearly double the number of

passengers allowed by the regulations, but
that at the very moment he came up with
it, he himself was stopped by an individual
who pretended that he, the constable, owed
him money and that by the time the mistake
was explained, the cab was out of sight.
Viewed by the light of subsequent evidence
we may take the statement for what it was
worth, seeing that his efforts to stop the cab
on the return journey when it was empty
had been equally futile 'in virtue of its
breakneck pace' to quote the constable's own
words. He was enabled, though, to distinguish the driver's uniform as belonging to
the 'Compagnie des Petites Voitures ;' not
a very difficult thing to do, there being at
the time only two associations of the kind in
Paris, and few if any 'pirates.' Both the
dress of the drivers and the carriages of the
rival companies were as conspicuously different in colour then as they are at the
present day.

According to Burns, the devil when

Francis Grosse was a-dying, refused to take him because he was such a damnable load; the Jehu of the 'Petites Voitures' does not seem to have had similar objections with regard to the taking of human over-weight to a place of martyrdom. As the reader proceeds he will gradually become aware that there is a great deal of unexplained mystery in this 'Masterly Début'; perhaps the most unaccountable aspect of it is the conduct and attitude of the driver Bardot. The French law of evidence is altogether different from the English, and many a French witness has before now been kept in solitary confinement for weeks because the *juge d'instruction* could not bend him to his will; *i.e.*, could not get him to implicate the prisoner whom said *juge* had made up his mind to send for trial. To those who watched this case from the beginning, Bardot looked much more like a willing accomplice than an independent witness or an unconscious accessory before the fact, yet, he was allowed to remain at large during the whole of the preliminary investigation, nor was there the least attempt to indict him after the trial. True, his evidence, as far as it went, was apparently straightforward enough, but one could not help being struck with its too deliberate ingenuousness, Dogberry's 'do not forget to specify, when time and place shall serve, that I am an ass,' is as nothing to Bardot's anxiety to be considered a drivelling idiot.

For instance, the fact of being hailed at past twelve at night by a party of seven to take them a distance of five or six miles does not surprise Bardot; he drives as a matter of course to the little station of Pantin where the young man who has hired him descends, accompanied by the woman and two of her children, leaving him, the cabman, in charge of the other three. His principal fare, point-ing to a dead wall a couple of hundred yards away and slightly visible in the light of the fitful moon, simply tells him that that is their destination. He has scarcely turned his back before he descends from his seat and for want of something better to do begins to talk to the children. By his own confession he asked the little ones the reason of this nocturnal journey. The reply, though somewhat startling, does not startle him. 'We don't know,' says the eldest, 'our friend Troppmann is taking us to our father, by our father's directions.' In his first account, however, Bardot does not give the name as we have written it, he slurs it, pretending that he did not catch it distinctly. His hearing does not seem to have been quite so defective in other respects, for he volunteers the statement that his conversation with the children was interrupted once or twice by cries of distress and the violent barking of dogs coming from the direction in which the other party and their guide had gone; cries perfectly

audible notwithstanding, or perhaps because
of the high wind that prevailed. And yet,
this very honest witness does not make the
slightest comment upon what he has heard
when the young man returns alone to claim
the other three children, merely saying
curtly; 'You can go. We have made up
our minds to stay.' He merely pockets his
money and travels back as fast as possible;
he denies that he has been ordered to stop
on his return journey by the policeman
alluded to above, or rather in order not to
commit himself he pretends not to have
heard the order, he, whose defective hearing
did not prevent his hearing the cries of
distress at least four or five hundred
yards away, seeing that the dead wall to
which the young man pointed was midway
between the Pantin Railway Station and
the freshly dug grave. And to crown the
whole, though Paris has been ringing with
the account of the crime for at least forty-
eight hours, Bardot after giving his first

evidence, is utterly astonished at being told of the *involuntary* part he has played in the tragedy, for he avers ' that up till then he has not heard a word of it.' A driver, plying about the streets of the capital from morn till night, and reading the papers in his enforced waits for custom has remained in utter ignorance of ' the Pantin Murder ' of which everyone has been talking, of which the papers are full.

Moreover, do what he will, Bardot cannot remember the name told him by the children, he will not even be certain that it is not a Christian name, nor is he positive that the little one said ' our friend.' He may have misunderstood altogether; ' the wind was so high.' Consequently when M. Claude, the head of the detective force starts for Havre to interrupt the possible flight across the seas of the murderer, he is under the impression that he is running after Jean Kinck, the matricide and fratricide, not after Jean Baptiste Troppmann of whose existence, let alone of his name, he is utterly ignorant. He has already telegraphed to the various seaports to keep a sharp look out for all suspicious characters on outgoing vessels, but his personal journey has been determined by the information of one of his subalterns, who maintains that the original of the photograph found upon the murdered woman has been seen by him, the detective, something like four-and-twenty hours after the crime was committed at the ' Taverne Anglaise,' a somewhat shady haunt for foreigners of all nationalities in the Rue Grange-Batelière (near the Old Opera). He had not seen the portrait then and the young fellow was furthermore muffled up, but he followed him and his companion to the Western Station and only left them when they had taken train.

When M. Claude reached Havre, the bird had been caged—though by sheer accident. The Rue Royale at Havre is simply a kind of French Ratcliff-Highway, it is the resort of sailors of all nations, who spend their hard-earned substance and indulge in amusements much in the same manner as they do on the banks of the Thames. During the latter years of the Second Empire, the ordinary *Sergent de ville* was replaced at the seaports by the *gendarme maritime*, and one of the latter, named Ferrand, noticing several suspicious looking individuals seated in one of the taverns, asked them for their names and passports. Theoretically he had no right to do so, for passports had been abolished in France, but when a policeman, either in France or elsewhere, takes it into his head to 'run' you in, the most sensible thing is to submit to his decision and to explain your position to his superiors. Had the individuals thus singled out by Ferrand done this, the chances would have been ten to one on their being set at liberty there and then, because neither Ferrand nor his superiors had the remotest idea that they had laid hands on the young fellow so urgently wanted by the Paris police for the Pantin murder. Instead of which, he, the young fellow, moved by fear made himself the spokesman of his companions and virtually drew all Ferrand's attention upon himself. 'I am a foreigner,' he said, turning very white and uncomfortable, 'and I was not aware that passports are necessary now-a-days in France.'

It was the most injudicious reply he could have made, for, coupled with his embarrassment it virtually increased the suspicion of the *gendarme* who insisted on taking him to the commissary. The first blunder is followed by a second, for no sooner is he on the quay than he manages to free himself of his captor by jumping into the water, apparently with the idea of committing suicide. His design is, however, frustrated by a ship-calker named Hanguel who jumps after him, and succeeds in bringing him to the shore, albeit that he nearly loses his life in the attempt, the drowning man doing his utmost to drag his would-be saviour to the bottom with him. When he is landed at last he is so exhausted as to have to be conveyed to the hospital, where he lies hovering betwixt life and death for nearly four-and-twenty hours. Then and then only the police become aware of the importance of their capture, though they are still ignorant of the whole of the truth, the prisoner's papers, carefully concealed beneath his shirt pointing him out as Jean Kinck, coming from Roubaix. In fact, M. Claude, who immediately on his arrival has been informed of all this, is still under the impression that he is dealing with the son and brother of Madame Kinck and her children.

To the detective's amazement, though his prisoner tells him that his name is not Jean Kinck, that Jean Kinck is not the son and brother of the murdered woman and the children, but the husband and father, that the eldest son whose name is Gustave and his sire are already on their way to America

under different names and that he, Jean
Baptiste Troppmann, their accomplice, but
not the actual murderer, is merely the
custodian of their papers.

It is at this point that the struggle
between M. Claude and Troppmann begins,
a struggle in which at first the clever
detective looks like getting the worst, a
struggle which justifies our title of 'A
Masterly Début,' for Troppmann himself
never loses his head for a single moment
and is very nigh persuading M. Claude—at
anyrate for a little while—that the criminal
must be looked for across the Atlantic. I
speak from personal knowledge, not from
hearsay, for I knew M. Claude for several
years, though perhaps not so well as I knew
one of his cleverest successors, M. Macé;
and he, M. Claude, declared more than once
that of all the criminals with whom he came
in contact during his career, only two fairly
astonished him by their imperturbable
sang-froid, namely, de la Pommeraies and

Troppmann. The fashionable Paris physician and French prototype of Pritchard was, however, apart from the coolness begotten from his profession, a much older and better-bred man than the Alsatian stripling, and yet, the latter was undoubtedly his superior as far as self-control and clever acting went. Madame de Pauw's murderer lost his temper on several occasions during his interviews with that most marvellous of all *juges d'instruction*, M. de Gonet; Troppmann from the moment he is in custody up to the last never gives himself away, though he has to stand much more formidable ordeals than the other. The first and most formidable one, after he has reached Paris, taxes all his resources as an actor, yet he is fully equal to it; to such a degree, in fact, as to make all the minor actors and spectators stand aghast. Not a muscle of his face moves when he is suddenly and without the slightest warning confronted with the bodies of his victims. He simply stares at them without as much as lifting his cap as the most inveterate French atheist would do in the presence of the dead; there is no tremor in his voice as he replies to the *juge d'instruction*'s question whether he can indentify the bodies laid out before him.

'Yes, monsieur,' he says, taking a few steps towards the marble slabs on which they are lying, and reciting their names as he points them out with his forefinger. Then he turns away as unconcerned as ever.

It is only when asked to sign the report of the proceedings in the adjoining room that he shows some hesitation; yet, he signs after all, protesting, however, that he has been only the instrument of Jean Kinck and his eldest son, Gustave. More than that the *juge* cannot draw from him, although the interview lasts for nearly two hours; at the end of which the prisoner is taken to Mazas. In reply to the oft-reiterated question whether he has any accomplices his last words are: 'Perhaps;' then looking his interlocutor full in the face, he adds : ' But you will not find them ; you will have to be satisfied with me only ' (*c'est assez de moi*).

In spite of all that has been subsequently said to the contrary, the prosecution was decidedly inclined at first to act upon the theory that Troppmann had accomplices. It seemed barely possible to the authorities that a mere stripling—and Troppmann was no more—could have accomplished the fiend-ish work that had been accomplished in so short a time. From that to the belief in the possible truth of Troppmann's as-severation that he was only the instru-ment of Jean Kinck and his eldest son, it wanted but a slight step ; consequently messages were dispatched to nearly all the American ports to keep a sharp look out for the missing Kincks. It is due to the memory of the clever detective to say that he was somewhat sceptical with regard to the wisdom of these messages ; he main-tained throughout that Jean and Gustave

Kinck had to be looked for, not in the land of the living, whether on this or on the other side of the Atlantic, but in some secluded spot beneath the sod; and when six days after the discovery of the six bodies, that of Gustave was unearthed close to the graves of his mother, brothers and sister, Claude prevailed upon his superiors to cease all inquiries abroad. He undertook to drag from Troppmann the secret of the whereabouts of Jean Kinck's remains, notwithstanding the former's assertion that, as far as he knew, the father was alive and must have murdered his eldest son, after the latter had assisted him in disposing of the rest of the family

From that moment Troppmann preserved an even more rigid silence than before on the crimes themselves, though he was willing enough to converse freely on any other subject with the four 'informers' by whom he was surrounded and among whom was Souvras, a very intelligent sub-inspector in the detective force. M. Claude looked upon the latter as his right hand, but I feel certain, notwithstanding all that has been said to the contrary subsequently, that Souvras proved of little use in this instance. The authorities felt well enough that without Jean Kinck, dead or alive, the evidence against Troppmann would be incomplete; but though Langlois' field was turned over in all directions,—no trace of the body was found.   Then M. Claude decided upon changing the basis of his investigations. From the very outset there was no doubt in M. Claude's mind that greed had been the motive of Troppmann's crime; and yet, neither money nor valuables were found upon him at the moment of his arrest when he was about to leave France, probably for ever. If he had succeeded in robbing Jean Kinck before or after doing away with him, what had he, Troppmann, done with the money. Assuredly not entrusted it to some one else. Nor did it appear that

Madame Kinck carried any important sum upon her when she arrived in Paris with her children.

The Kincks, it had been ascertained, were in easy, if not affluent circumstances. In Roubaix, where they lived, the head of the family who was connected with some engine-works there, was considered a 'safe man,' though far from a lavish one. He was not a native of the place, but like Troppmann, an Alsatian, and thanks to their common origin, as well as to their similarity of pursuits, a friendship had sprung up between them. In how far this bond had been strengthened by relations at which one dare scarcely hint in print or speech, had better remain a matter of conjecture in these pages, albeit that several eminent criminal lawyers and medical experts concurred in taking those relations for granted. Be this as it may, they had not the effect of making Jean Kinck unloosen his purse strings. From the accounts of those who frequently observed the elder Kinck and his companion at the café in Roubaix they were in the habit of patronising, the former remained persistently deaf to the latter's repeated laments about the lack of ready money wherewith to pursue his schemes, and this, notwithstanding Kinck's knowledge, that the elder Troppmann was a kind of genius in his way, that the son had inherited a good deal of the father's capacity and that he would not be scrupulous in appropriating the latter's secrets to his own use.   Virtually it was a case of Greek *versus* Greek, probably with the reservation in Jean Kinck's mind that he would not go to the length of murdering Troppmann.   But after all I have read since the trial I have no hesitation in saying that the smug and snug bourgeois of Roubaix would have had no scruples in flinging off Troppmann, after he had mastered the latter's secrets, or rather the elder Troppmann's, but for that *unspeakable* bond between him and the son to which I have already alluded, and to which perforce I may be compelled to allude again. Troppmann himself was probably aware of this; unable to extract the smallest sum from Jean Kinck's pockets, he made up his mind one day to have the whole of his property.

A few months after Troppmann's first appearance in Roubaix, he and Jean Kinck were missing from the latter's usual haunts and it was soon ascertained that both had gone on a journey to Alsace. A little while after that, Mrs Kinck in virtue of powers sent to her by her husband from that province began to realise their property, telling her friends and acquaintances that she was to proceed shortly with her family to America whither her husband would precede her, hence, the first statement of Troppmann when he was arrested—that Kinck and his eldest son were on their way to the United States would have borne a semblance of truth but for the discovery of the latter's body

As a matter of course, after that discovery, not the slightest credit was attached to Troppmann's words and the next logical step on the part of the police was to explore Alsace for traces of Jean Kinck, dead or alive. Their great difficulty, however, was to confine their research to the zone likely to yield practical results, or rather to find that zone, because Troppmann refused to give information upon the subject. He seemed bent, as it were, upon irritating and baffling his gaolers, with that vanity, so common to great (?) malefactors he was proud of 'leading them by the nose;' and notwithstanding all that has been said to the contrary, but for a fortuitous circumstance, Jean Kinck would have mouldered away undiscovered in the quiet nook where he was interred by his assassin. In this, as in other cases, the press was eminently useful to the authorities ; the press always will be, provided editors will control every statement and comment of their contributors, provided they, the editors, will refuse to be treated as schoolboys by the high and mighty members of the detective force, who—as a rule—have as much intelligence as would suffice for the *inefficient* management of a newspaper one day out of the three hundred and sixty-five. The editor should in all cases insist upon ungarbled information from head-quarters and it should be left to his sense of honour and responsibility to decide the shape and manner of publication. If a decoy paragraph be distributed or communicated, the editor and the editor alone should be informed of its fictitious nature. Such or nearly such was the system adopted by Canler, and we have yet to learn that the English or for that matter any other detective force has produced a cleverer man than he was. I am essentially averse to 'beating about the bush' whether in print or in speech. I have seen a good deal of the undercurrents of 'detective practice,' especially of so-called 'private detective practice,' during a very long spell of journalism both at home and abroad and am not likely to have penned the above without good foundations.

Upon the face of it there was no reason why Jean Kinck, whether successful or not in benefiting by the schemes set afoot, or apparently set afoot, by Troppmann, should wish to rid himself of his wife and children,—upon the face of it only. We must beg the reader to remember that from the very commencement of the inquiry there was sufficient evidence of the existence of mysterious relations between the assassin and his first victim which could not possibly be made public without outraging public decency. The pathologists and physiologists deemed those relations a very strong motive for the murder of his family by Jean Kinck, and Troppmann, far from denying the motive, confirmed it. Nay, more; he had laid his plans so carefully with that view before the murders

that among the documents found in Kinck's
house at Roubaix, there was a letter which
contained strong circumstantial evidence
that such relations existed. Consequently,
the body of Jean Kinck or the live man
had to be found at all costs. M. Claude's
men had been scouring Alsace for several
days in all directions, but without the
slightest result when the postmaster at
Guebviller, having seen an account of the
case in the papers, made a communication
to the authorities.

As I have already stated, that shortly after
Jean Kinck's departure with Troppmann for
Alsace, Madame Kinck began to realise her
husband's property, probably by the latter's
directions and that the lawyer entrusted
with the transaction deposed to having
handed to Mrs Kinck part of the proceeds,
namely 5000 francs. What had become of
these? They were not re-invested in
Roubaix; on the other hand, Mrs Kinck's
well-known frugal habits precluded all idea

of her having spent them, and they were not found upon her body. Troppmann, when apprehended, possessed little or no money. When interrogated on the subject, he at first opposed an obstinate silence, then at last, in a cleverly simulated burst of anger, he exclaimed : 'Leave me alone, you either can't or won't see that Kinck had the money and that he has taken it to America with him.'

The money, however, had not been carried to America, either in the pockets of Jean Kinck or of any one else ; it was simply lying at the post-office at Guebviller until Jean Kinck should claim it *personally*. It had been claimed already twice, in both cases with discomfiture to the claimants. The first time it was Troppmann himself, who provided with all the documents necessary to such a claim, applied for the letter, which had not only been addressed *poste-restante*, but registered besides. Had he succeeded in obtaining it, the lives of Gustave Kinck, his mother and his brothers and sister would probably have been safe. But of all improbabilities the most improbable happened, and though Messrs Sims, Buchanan, Pettitt and the minor stars of that school are allowed considerable latitude by their audiences in the selection of coincidences, a coincidence such as that which really happened, if invented by them, would be unhesitatingly rejected. The postmaster at Guebviller had been a schoolfellow, or if not that, a chum, of Jean Kinck, and met Troppmann's demand for the letter with the remark that Kinck was a man of twice Troppmann's age, that, consequently, he could not give him that letter. 'Surely,' he added, 'you do not pretend to be Jean Kinck?' To which question Troppmann failed to give a reply; he merely slunk out of the place without attempting to explain.

It were idle to speculate upon the steps that would have commended themselves, under such circumstances, to any responsible official whether English or foreign. Experience has taught us before now, not to pin our faith on the intelligence of the average employé of any great organisation ; Percy Lefroy was allowed to walk out of the Brighton station unmolested when the most elementary logic would have prescribed his detention ; Troppmann caught in the act of personating Jean Kinck was allowed to leave the place , and when a few days later Gustave Kinck applies for that same letter, but in his own name, saying what he probably believes to be the truth, that his father's hurried departure for Paris has prevented him from applying himself, the postmaster, although refusing to part with the dispatch, lets matters rest there. He takes no steps to elucidate what, to use the mildest term, must have seemed to him a strange affair, until the newspaper accounts of the murders in Paris and the conjectures as to the fate of Jean Kinck himself stare him positively in the face. Then and then only he volunteers the information, which, if given a few weeks previously might have preserved seven innocent victims from the fate of a perhaps not altogether blameless one.

The postmaster's information was doubly useful to the authorities in that it not only disposed of Troppmann's contention that Jean Kinck had gone off with the money to America after having murdered his family, but that it virtually localised the area of search for Kinck's body—for the idea of finding Jean Kinck alive was from that moment abandoned as altogether chimerical. In fairness to M. Claude, it should be said that he had not waited until then to dispatch his men to Alsace, but they had gone to work at random, and though they had found a pair of trousers stained with blood in the neighbourhood of Obviller, they failed to discover any traces of the man to whom the garment was supposed to have belonged It was afterwards proved that this had been one of the masterly tricks of Troppmann to throw the police off the scent, because in reality not a drop of blood was shed in the taking Jean Kinck's life.

Nevertheless, even with something more definite to go upon than they had hitherto, the efforts of the police would have proved fruitless, though they must have been at least a score of times within a few yards from the spot where Jean Kinck lay buried, but for a flock of crows which took flight at their approach to the ruins of the castle of Herrenfluch.

This time, their guide, a native of those parts and probably a kind of 'mute inglorious' White of Selborne or Bewick maintained that the foregathering of such a number of sable-winged scavengers betokened the existence of a mass of putrifying flesh somewhere in the immediate vicinity. The conclusion that this putrifying mass had been human once, was not difficult to arrive at, seeing that there were no traces of it above ground, and that, as a rule, people do not bury the carcasses of animals which are not deemed worth the trouble of removal. And in fact, notwithstanding the advance of the exploring party, a few of those funereal-looking birds obstinately kept their ground until the human beings were within a stone's throw, then with dismal croaking, perched in the trees overhead, without, however, relinquishing their carrion.

At the same time the guide caught a glimpse of something bright glistening in the sun through a crevice in a large heap of stones ; in a few moments the stones are scattered and two human feet protruding from the loosely - trodden soil revealed to the gaze of the excited spectators. The murderer has not even taken the trouble to bury his victim properly. From the very first the identity of the murdered man scarcely admits of a doubt, one of the Paris detectives declares the socks on the corpse's feet to be of the same material and pattern as those worn by the male members of the Kinck family. Not a speck of blood was visible anywhere. Troppmann afterwards confessed that he had merely mixed a few drops of prussic acid with the contents of his pocket flask, and watched for the opportunity of Kinck being thirsty to offer him the poisoned liquor. The opportunity had presented itself amidst the ruins of Herrenfluch one sultry autumn afternoon. The body had been buried where it fell, there was no need for any struggle, nor was there any appearance of one.

This much may be stated with confidence, the rest, including Troppmann's version of his having fabricated the poison himself will probably remain a matter of more or less intelligent conjecture to the very end. One thing, though, is very certain, Troppmann, endowed as he was with marvellous strength and agility, could not possibly have dispatched his last six victims by himself and buried them in the short time alleged by the prosecution, even if their grave had been dug beforehand in the almost equally incredibly short space mentioned in the indictment. In vain did that eminent barrister, Maitre Georges Lachaud, senior, endeavour to point all this out at the trial, the authorities were determined to look for no accomplices, and Troppmann stood alone in the dock when he should have stood there with at least two or three others. Nay more, the prosecution was so evidently bent upon implicating Troppmann and Troppmann only that it endeavoured to impart a fictitious air of strength to his face by refusing him to be shaved during the whole of his preliminary incarceration. As a consequence, the accused 'on the morning of his trial, looked considerably older and more vigorous that he really was, albeit that, as I have already said, he was vigorous to a degree. When at last, at the imperative demand of his counsel, the beard and moustache were taken off, the spectators beheld a stripling whom to suspect and accuse of

all those monstrous crimes seemed but little
short of a farce.   In short, the whole of this
affair, the way in which it was conducted,
the suppression of evidence, material to the
issue, not as far as Troppmann himself was
concerned, but in the interest of public
justice and morality, point to it as one of
the mysteries of which the Second Empire
was so fruitful.

As a matter of course, Troppmann was
sentenced and executed. Those who saw
him in his last moments, and I was one of
them, could not deny him his courage; notwithstanding all that has been said to the
contrary, he neither budged nor winced
while they cut his hair, which had been
allowed to grow, and the collar of his shirt.
He steadfastly refused to name his accomplices, though insisting all the while that
he had not struck the fatal blows.

A JOINT-MASTERPIECE

LESS than a twelvemonth after the execution of Billoir for the murder of Marie Le Manach, Paris was startled one day by the report of a similar crime having been committed. Two human arms and two human thighs had been found in a *garni* in the Rue Poliveau, near the Zoological Gardens. The surgeon attached to the police division declared those remains to be those of a woman.

They were found in a room which, according to the proprietor of the Hôtel Jeanson, had been occupied the last time before the discovery by two young fellows, the one dark, the other fair. The former had inscribed his name on the register as 'Emile Gérard, age twenty-six, student, from Blois.' A fortnight had elapsed since they had slept there—for one night only—and but for the necessity of cleaning and dusting a cupboard for a lodger who intended to take up his quarters permanently at the Hôtel Jeanson, the severed limbs might have remained hidden for months.   They were wrapped up in some old Oxford shirting and a black petticoat, and furthermore tied up in that peculiar packing paper, which is brown on one side and coated with tar on the other.

The Paris *Figaro* was the first to publish these details, for the *Figaro* had not waited for the confirmation of the report by the police to send one of its representatives to the spot.   The *Figaro* has had for years and has still on its staff an able journalist whose special and almost exclusive duty it is to keep his eyes and ears wide open for the faintest rumour or the vaguest indication of a crime. That such a man who, as a rule, is far higher endowed than the ordinary detective, should be able to give the latter a hint now and then, need not be said; and nine cases out of ten the Paris detective is not above taking it. In this instance, however, the auxiliaries of M. Jacob maintained that the *Figaro* had been hoaxed, that the whole affair was nothing more nor less than the practical joke of some medical students, that the remains were simply limbs, subtracted from the dissecting rooms at Clamart, and in order to substantiate their argument, they cited the opinion of several surgeons who declared that the 'cutting up' had been done too scientifically to be the work of any but a thoroughly practical anatomist.

The *Figaro* stuck to its text and was supported in its views by such eminent authorities as Doctors Bergeron, Delens and Brouardel, the latter, perhaps, the most eminent lecturer on what the French call

' forensic medicine,' what we call ' medical jurisprudence.' These gentlemen averred that though there was evidence of some skill, the skill was that of an intelligent butcher, or at best of a dissector of animals, not of human bodies. This, as we shall see presently, ought to have provided the police with some clue, however slight, but it did not. They were determined to treat the whole affair as a clever piece of mystification and it being the beginning of April they asserted with a sneer that, in order to throw the *Figaro* off its guard, the attempt to make ' an April Fool' of the paper, had been postponed from the 1st to the 6th, the date of the discovery.

M. Guillot, an essentially clever *juge d'instruction* was inclined to side with the *Figaro*, but, at the same time, he could not entirely ignore the opinion of his subordinates, so he hit upon a sensible way of conciliating both parties. ' If this be merely a joke,' he said, ' Emile Gérard ought to be punished severely for bringing his profession into contempt. I doubt whether the law would enable me to do so, but if I can catch him, I can keep him in durance vile for a fortnight or so, while I pretend to inquire into the matter. That will be a lesson to him.'

Consequently a warrant was issued against said Emile Gérard, and M. Jacob published a detailed description of the limbs, especially of one arm which had on it a seton bound up with an ivy leaf.

As in the case of Billoir's victim the number of relatives and friends pretending to verify the limb as belonging to their nearest and dearest is legion, meanwhile the news spreads that Emile Gérard has been arrested.

The individual apprehended turns out to be a M. Bernard, by profession, a waiter, by inclination a Don Juan, who has assumed the name in order to avoid complications at home where reigns a jealous wife. He has never been to the Hôtel Jeanson, but has occupied an apartment in a neighbouring hotel with a rival to his legal spouse. His incarceration at Mazas, he complained afterwards, was the least of his punishment for his infidelity.

Nor does the comic element in the crime of the Rue Poliveau end there. A few days later *La Petite Presse* prints the following sensational article :—

A CLUE

The Two Assassins Revisit the Scene of their Crime in the Rue Poliveau— Where is the Driver of the Cab?

'On Thursday at twenty minutes to six, a hackney cab drawn by a dapple - grey stopped before the tobacconist and wine shop of Madame Noël, at No. 30 Rue de Poliveau, consequently almost opposite the Hôtel Jeanson.

'Two individuals alighted from the cab,

entered the shop and bought some cigars at 25 centimes a piece. Madame Noël noticed the excited appearance of her customers and she avers having heard the shorter of the two say in a whisper. "We bought some cigars here on the day we brought the limbs." After which they left the shop hurriedly and got into the cab which drove off.

'The shorter of the two was very neatly dressed in a short overcoat, black jacket and brown trousers. He wore a tall hat, was very dark and quick in his movements. He seemed restless and could scarcely keep still for a moment. The taller one wore a billy-cock and a brown suit with a kind of ulster over it. He had a heavy, reddish moustache.

'Madame Noël felt so utterly stupified at what she had heard that she allowed the two wretches to get away. It was only when the cab had driven off that she be-thought herself to acquaint the detectives who were watching in the Rue de Poliveau for the return of the criminal to the spot where the crime *has not* been committed, with what had occurred.

'The detectives did their utmost, but failed to come up with the cab. Their prey had escaped.

'At the time of our going to press, the cabman has probably been found and has given the authorities the necessary information.

'The culprits are not arrested yet, but suspicion has already grown into certainty, the net is being drawn closer around them, and by to-morrow the police will have the criminals in its power. Then it will be its duty to act with less haste, so as to capture the accessories before and after the fact, and to dispel with one stroke the mystery surrounding this horrible plot.

'Hence we appeal to everyone to afford the police such information as may lead to the further elucidation of the facts pointed out by us. The Rue de Poliveau is a very solitary street, and the very fact of having driven two individuals to Madame Noël's shop must have struck the driver, whosoever he be.'"

Meanwhile the two men who had caused all this excitement were quietly doing their work in their respective offices, for they were simply two journalists who had been to the Hôtel Jeanson in search of copy, and while still full of their subject had stopped at Madame Noël's to buy some cigars. One of them had said to the other, 'I should not feel surprised, if it transpired that they actually came here to buy some cigars before depositing their parcels.' The two journalists were MM. Monréal of the *Nouveau Journal*, and Friedlander of *Le Petit Parisien.**

And though they contributed nothing to the *dénouement* of the drama, the culprits would have probably escaped their fate but

* I had the story from the latter gentleman, with whom, during my stay in Paris, I was on excellent terms.

for the obstinacy of another journalist, a very smart and bustling reporter on the staff of *La Liberté*.

Peyrocave had made up his mind to get at the identity of the victim. In following up a clue, Peyrocave had the tenacity of purpose with which Eugène Sue endowed that Englishman who followed the lion tamer from place to place in the hope of seeing him rent to pieces by one of his animals. Peyrocave managed to infect the police with his enthusiasm and he and they began by scouring every quarter of Paris, inquiring of people as they went whether any of their female friends were missing. Theoretically this was an almost impossible task to undertake, in reality it was not very formidable, though it was formidable enough. Though the arms found in the cupboard of the Hôtel Jeanson were plump, the hands attached to them were wrinkled and hard, showing that their owner was a bee, and not a drone in

the hive of humanity; there was, moreover, the seton of which I have already
spoken. The medical experts stated, furthermore, that the limbs belonged to a woman
no longer young. Putting this and that
together, Peyrocave, who probably knew
the seamy side of Paris life better than the
bright side, came to the conclusion that the
woman had been decoyed and murdered for
her money by one of those Lovelaces of the
pavement with which Paris teems; for he
was well aware that there is no fool like an
old fool, whether it be a man or a woman,
when his or her amorous passions are aroused.
Peyrocave was too experienced a Paris
reporter to eliminate the elements of greed
and so-called love from his calculations—for
the Paris reporter is an essentially different
creature from the Fleet Street one, there is
no tacit compact between him and Mrs
Grundy, 'not to stir mud, even in the
interests of justice.' Peyrocave knew that,
especially among the softer sex, there are

many who in their soberer moments might take themselves to task for being such fools, but who do not, and simply become reckless with their hard-won earnings when they take a fancy to some handsome, though low-bred scoundrel, who bleeds them pecuniarily. or failing to do which, bleeds them literally to death.

Hence, Peyrocave's inquiries were based upon the assumption that the murdered woman was ' no better than she should have been,' and that her murderer was a some-time lover. Peyrocave was only wrong in one of his surmises. Among the women whose reputation was far from spotless. and who had been missing for some weeks from their neighbourhood was a Madame Gillet. She was a milkseller—which does not imply that she kept a dairy—and reputed to have amassed a considerable hoard. Further inquiries elicited the fact that she had a seton on her arm, and the black petticoat in which the limbs were wrapped was identified by Madame Grand, an old friend and country-woman of hers, as having been usually worn by Madame Gillet.

To show that Peyrocave had proceeded upon the basis laid down by the greatest of French detectives, we may mention that immediately following this discovery, several former lovers of Madame Gillet were arrested without result, however, for the proprietor of the Hôtel Jeanson failed to recognise any of them.

It gradually leaked out though, that shortly before her death or disappearance, Madame Gillet had had some transactions or attempts at transactions, with a young fellow of the name of Barré, who had been originally a lawyer's clerk, but had started in business for himself as a rent and debt collector, valuer, commission agent, etc., etc. I am trying to give the English equivalents for that kind of occupation, the followers of which in France dub themselves "*hommes d'affai*." I doubt, however, whether the thing itself and the man exist among us to the same extent they exist in France. Our working classes do not hoard as they do in France, nor is the spirit of speculation so rife among them. Least of all have they the constant expectation of some windfall in the shape of a legacy from some rich relative, 'upon whom it would be well to keep their eyes;' in short, the conditions of life are altogether different.

It was never accurately ascertained whether Madame Gillet had made the acquaintance of Barré through one of her neighbours, Madame Seurin, a somnambulist—if you please—and the proprietress of a registry office for servants, or whether, as in the case of Bella Marks and Lord Beaufoy in 'School,' the milk jug had been the means of improving their relations; one thing was certain though: shortly after Madame Gillet's disappearance, Barré moved from his domicile and office in the Rue Hauteville to more modest and distant quarters in the Rue Rochebrunne, where he was arrested. As a matter of course, he opposed a stout denial to any and every charge. When confronted with the proprietress of the Hôtel Jeanson, the latter failed to identify him, but Barré was kept in custody for all that, because M. Guillot, in this instance, had acted upon something stronger than mere suspicion.

Barré had been in Paris four years, during part of which time he had been employed by two solicitors as fourth and third clerk. While in the former position he became acquainted with a man of the name of Demol, an old soldier, who had been decorated on the battlefield. He was the trusted messenger of Barré's principal and had, moreover, the charge of a house in the Rue Monge, as *concierge*. Barré often entrusted him with private messages, and when he left did not lose sight of him, but continued to employ him as heretofore. When Demol read of the identification of Madame

Gillet's limbs, he went straight to M. Guillot and communicated his suspicions. His evidence showed conclusively that Barré who previous to the latter end of March had been exceedingly 'tight' for money, so 'tight' as to be compelled to borrow of him, Demol, had all at once become very flush, paid most of his debts and negotiated several valuable securities. He, moreover, deposed to having waited for twenty minutes on one occasion for Barré in a cab, while the latter went to pay a visit to a friend, a student in the Quartier-Latin. 'I am sorry to have kept you so long,' Barré had said on his return, 'but my friend is so busy that I had to wait until he could spare a moment. You would be surprised at the number of human limbs he has in his room for dissecting purposes, and what is stranger still, his mistress who is living with him, does not seem frightened in the least.'

Two days after the conversation Demol accompanied Barré to the Temple to buy a small trunk, which he, Barré, wanted 'to send some clothes to his mistress at Angers.' Demol, in fact, knew that when Barré first came from Angers he was accompanied by a girl who had a child by him.

It had been ascertained, by that time, that Madame Gillet was possessed of about 20,000 francs, mostly invested in 'municipal bonds.' The numbers of some of these were known, through the gossip of the neighbours, to whom she had shown them, but the communication of these numbers to the money changers and stock jobbers of the capital failed to bring the securities to light, and it was not until Demol gave additional information in that respect that M. Guillot felt on safe ground. Then and then only he unmasked all his batteries with the prisoner.

The latter did not surrender at once. He admitted having negotiated the securities belonging to Madame Gillet, but en-

deavoured to show that they had been
entrusted to him in order to get an advance
upon, and that he had merely appropri-
ated the proceeds. As for his client, he
denied all knowledge of her whereabouts or
of her fate. During the whole of a day
M. Guillot failed in every attempt to draw
Barré out, but the next, he all of a sudden
abandoned his system of denying every-
and exclaimed :—

'Very well, I am guilty, but I was driven
to it by an accomplice.'

'Will you tell me his name ?'

'Yes, seeing that it is all over with me.
I'll have company at any rate, his name is
Lebiez.'

'Where does he live ?'

'In the Quartier-Latin.'

'Near the Rue Poliveau.'

'Yes, near the Rue Poliveau, in the Rue
des Fossés Saint Jacques, in a *hôtel garni*.'

'What is his profession ?'

'He is attached to the anatomical depart-

ment of the Zoological Gardens; it is he
who disected the body.'

'You helped him?'

'No.'

'But you went with him to the Rue
Poliveau, it was you who wrote on a card
the name of Emile Gérard?'

'It was I?'

'Where did you hide the body?'

'In a trunk.'

'The trunk you made Demol buy for
you?'

'Yes, and we dispatched it to Le Mans?'

'Why did you do this?'

'Because we intended to go there our-
selves, and we should have scattered the
remains far and wide.'

'To what address did you send it?'

'To be left till called for.'*

In less than an hour after this conversa-

---

* I have reported this conversation from the notes of the secretary
of the *juge d'instruction* which were produced at the trial. I have
only to add that until that magistrate closes the case, as far as he is
concerned, no prisoner is allowed to have legal assistance.

tion, M. Jacob, accompanied by the commissary specially attached to the office of the Public Prosecutor, was on his way to Le Mans, where the legs, the head and trunk of Madame Gillet were found packed in the manner described by Barré.

Lebiez was arrested at his domicile the following morning. It was never satisfactorily proved that he was the instigator of the crime, though there could be no doubt of his complicity before and after the fact, but this very distinction made and makes him still the more interesting of the two, especially from a psychological point of view. Not for one, single moment did he lose his presence of mind. His attitude before, during and after the trial, up to the instant of his death reminds one irresistibly of Lacenaire's and to a certain extent of Ravachol's, who paid the penalty of his crimes only a few months ago. But he had received a higher education than either of these men. He was a freethinker and while the whole of Paris was in a state of frantic excitement consequent upon the discovery at the Hôtel Jeanson, he kept sufficiently cool to give a public lecture on 'Darwinism and the Church.' Nay, more, during the three weeks preceding his arrest when every resource of the detective force was strained to the utmost to let a gleam of light into this dark maze of crime, he ventured day after day into the Palais de Justice to transact some formal business in connection with a new paper, of which he was to be the responsible publisher. He did not deny having given Madame Gillet what were virtually the death blows in the region of the heart when the hammer with which Barré assailed her from behind in his lodgings in the Rue Hauteville failed to do its work at once. Yet, this man was by no means cruel. In the neighbourhood where he lived the children doted on him, on the day of his arrest the inmates and proprietor of the *hôtel garni*, a room of which he had occupied for months, scouted the idea of the guilt of a man 'who would not hurt a cat in spite of his profession,' as they put it.

While Madame Gillet's body was still warm, Barré took a key from her pocket and proceeded to her lodgings hard by to get possession of her securities. It transpired, on the evidence of Barré himself, that on his return, Lebiez did not so much as vouchsafe a question as to the amount of the spoil—if spoil it was, to him, seeing that it remained a matter of doubt to the last whether he had to any extent benefited pecuniarily by the crime. For Lebiez though not rich, appears to have been above want, and was, moreover, frugal in his habits.

'What then induced him to commit so foul a deed?' it will be asked. Such a question could only be answered by the highest authority on mental diseases, for in Lebiez we are confronted with the problem of the dual man in the flesh, the dual man as

represented to us by Mr Louis Stevenson in
'Dr Jekyll and Mr Hyde,' the dual man
of whom the world in general knows little
or nothing, unless his evil impulses should
bring him to the Assizes Courts, as they
brought thither Rafinat and Firon, the
woman Dubos and Jadin, the valet of the
Marquis de Hallays, and last but not least a
criminal whose name I have forgotten,
though I have a distinct recollection of
having read the case in an old file of the
Gazette des Tribunaux. It was a trial for
murder and rape committed at Saint Cyr
near Lyons. The circumstances were too
horrible to be narrated here, but one of the
prisoners maintained that there had been
not the least premeditation on his part,
seeing that he had been accidentally invited
to accompany the two principals in the
affair at the moment they were starting on
their errand of homicide. His statement was
proved to be substantially correct. He had
no knife or arms of any kind, he had merely

picked up on the way a large stone wherewith to help dispatching the victims. And when the presiding judge, struck by the justice of the remark asked him; 'But why, knowing that these men virtually invited you to commit murder, did you accompany them?' his answer was. 'Between neighbours, one feels bound to oblige one another.'

Did Lebiez feel bound to oblige Barré? It would be difficult to determine; certain is it that he did not bear the latter a grudge for having betrayed him and that he died game, very game, albeit that his agony was prolonged by several moments, his companion in crime taking precedence of him under the guillotine. Barré's courage forsook him at the last moment, Lebiez was staunch to the end, so staunch as to draw from a spectator the enthusiastic exclamation; 'Bravo, Lebiez.' The spectator was a printer residing in the suburbs, and a friend of the would-have-been publisher of the *Père Duchêne.*

THE END